CINDERS & SONG

WISPWATER VALLEY ROMANCES

ANNIKA STONE

978-1-943192-98-4

A

CINDERS & SONG

1

The bell woke her.

It wasn't a grand, tolling thing from a clock tower. Wispwater didn't have towers. It was a sharp, brassy handbell, rung with cheerful, annoying precision just on the other side of her garden fence.

Emil.

Petra buried her face deeper into the pillow. The wool scratch against her cheek was a kindness. The bed was warm. Her body, heavy and slow to wake, felt like a stone sinking into river mud.

She didn't move. Not yet.

Most people described the blacksmith as a force of nature—a woman who rose before the sun to beat the iron into submission. They imagined her silhouetted against the dawn, hammer raised, tireless.

It was a nice image. Heroic.

It was also a lie.

Petra slept late. She slept because forging "Gentle Iron"—iron that remembered its purpose, iron that held a roof against a storm or kept a gate latch true—took more than muscle. It took a piece of her own density. By evening, she was hollowed out. By morning, she was just barely heavy enough to be a person again.

Clang.

"Teacher," she mumbled into the mattress. "Stop."

He didn't stop. Emil never stopped. He was probably standing on the steps of the schoolhouse right now, sleeves rolled up despite the autumn chill, smiling at the children tumbling into the yard.

Petra rolled over. Her joints popped—a series of dry cracks, loud in the small room. Her knees ached. Her right shoulder, the hammer-shoulder, felt tight, a cable pulled to its limit.

She sat up.

The cottage was small, tucked behind the larger timber buildings of the village square like a boulder hiding behind a tree. It was built of the same grey stone as the valley floor, but softer inside. Detailed with wood she hadn't carved and rugs she hadn't woven. Trades. Her life was a collection of barters.

She stood, the floorboards cold under her bare feet.

Dressing was a ritual of armoring.

First, the linen shift, soft and worn thin.

Then the trousers—heavy wool, dyed dark grey, reinforced at the knees.

Then the shirt, thick flannel that buttoned to the chin.

She braided her hair back, her thick fingers moving clumsily with the fine strands. She tied it off with a leather thong. Finally, the boots. Heavy leather, steel-toed, laced tight.

She opened her front door.

The air hit her like a wet sheet. It was late autumn, the time of year when Wispwater held its breath between the harvest and the snow. Petra's cottage faced the back of the village green. To her right, just over a low stone wall, was the school yard.

She saw the children lining up—tiny bundles of wool and energy. She saw Emil, his back to her, lowering the brass handbell. He laughed at something a child said, a sound that carried clearer than the bell.

Petra stepped back into the shadows of her porch. She didn't want to be seen. Not yet. She wasn't ready to be the blacksmith. She was still just Petra, waking up.

She turned left, taking the narrow path that wound between the bakery and the weaver's shop, heading toward the edge of town.

The commute was her transition.

As she walked, she passed the things she had made.

The railing outside the weaver's shop—still smooth, no rust.

The hinges on the baker's delivery door—holding the heavy oak without sagging.

The scraper by the General Store—worn bright silver from years of muddy boots.

She didn't look at the people. She looked at the iron.

You holding? she asked the scraper.

I'm holding, the iron seemed to say.

The smithy was at the far end of the village, down where the cobblestones gave way to the packed earth of the stables and the inn. It made sense for it to be there—noise and smoke belonged on the perimeter, away from the sleeping babies and drying laundry.

The smithy was a squat building, hunkered down into the earth. It looked like a natural formation, a cave with a chimney and a weird wooden lean-to attached.

Petra walked up the slope. The smell hit her before she reached the door—coal dust and the deep, mineral scent of cold iron.

She pulled the heavy iron ring of the door. The hinges didn't creak—Petra's hinges never creaked—but the door swung outward with a heavy, pressurized sigh.

Inside, she lit the fire. This was the only gentle thing she did all day. A nest of kindling. A strike of flint. The catch of orange flame. She pumped the bellows, watching the heart of the forge wake up.

The heat bloomed. It pushed against her face, tight and stinging. Petra leaned into it. She closed her eyes. The fire woke up, and Petra finally, truly, arrived in her body.

The door opened behind her.

Petra didn't jump. She knew the vibration of those steps. Slow. Heavy. Deliberate.

Fen.

Petra turned.

The potter stood in the open doorway, outlined by the grey morning light. Tall, broad in the way an old oak tree is broad. They wore a canvas coat smeared with dried clay, the grey dust settled into the creases of their face and the silver of their hair.

"Fen," Petra said.

"Petra."

Fen's voice was like gravel rolling downhill. They stepped inside, closing the door specifically to cut the draft. Fen hated drafts. Clay dried too fast.

They walked to the cooling rack, hands clasped behind their back. They stopped in front of the gate latch for the miller.

Fen leaned in. They didn't touch it. They just looked.

Petra wiped her hands on her apron. She waited. A potter understood form. If Fen looked at it this long, something was there.

Fen turned their head slightly, listening.

"What?" Petra asked.

Fen reached out and tapped the iron with a fingernail.

Tink.

The sound was flat. Dead.

"It holds," Petra said, defensive heat rising. "The measurement is true, Fen."

Fen looked at her, their eyes the color of wet slate. "Cold."

"It's iron. Iron is cold."

"No," Fen said. "It's... quiet."

They picked up the latch. It was heavy, straight, perfect. But Fen held it like it was a dead bird. "The miller needs a latch that holds. This just... isn't."

Petra took it from them. She gripped the cold metal. The latch felt... empty. Just metal. The spark she usually felt—the hum of the fire trapped inside—was gone.

"It's the autumn," Petra said, putting it back. "The frost gets into the grain."

Fen didn't argue. They just reached into their pocket and pulled out a small, wrapped bundle.

"For the teacher," Fen said, placing it on the bench. A green mug. "He broke his."

Petra stared at it. "Emil?"

"He needs a new one. I thought... you're neighbors."

"You could walk it over, Fen. The school is right there."

Fen looked at their boots. "He's singing today. The handbell... it's loud."

Petra almost smiled. "He does that."

"Too much noise." Fen looked at her. "You take it."

It wasn't a request. Fen touched the "quiet" latch one last time.

"Iron waits, Petra," Fen said. "People don't."

They turned and left.

Petra stood alone in the orange glow. She looked at the latch.

She picked up her heaviest hammer. She needed noise. She needed to prove the iron still had a voice. She placed a bar of stock on the anvil and swung.

THUD.

The forge groaned. It sounded like it was in pain.

2

The walk home was harder than the walk there. In the morning, Petra was mostly just fighting gravity. In the evening, she was fighting the accumulation of the day. Every strike of the hammer, every lift of the tongs, every twist of the pliers—it all settled into her muscles like silt at the bottom of a riverbed.

By the time she clamped the final vise shut, the sun had already slipped behind the western ridge. The forge was cooling, ticking softly as the metal contracted.

Petra took off her apron. Stiff with soot and smelled of singed leather, it went back to its hook by the door. A heavy, shedding skin that she was glad to leave behind.

She picked up the basket from yesterday's dinner. It was waiting by the door, empty except for the gingham cloth Marda wanted back.

Then she hesitated.

She looked at the workbench. The green mug sat there, wrapped in Fen's rag.

Iron waits. People didn't

Petra sighed, a sound that scraped against the silence of the room. She picked up the mug and nestled it into the basket, tucking the cloth around it so it wouldn't rattle. She wasn't promising to deliver it. She was just... moving it closer.

Outside in the lean-to, she went to the pump in the corner, the one that fed the quenching troughs. The water came up directly from the deep aquifer, colder than snowmelt. She stuck her head under the spout and pumped.

The cold hit her scalp like a hammer blow. It washed the salt from her eyelashes and the grit from her neck. She sputtered, scrubbing at her arms with rapid, rough motions. She wasn't clean—she was never truly clean until Sunday—but she was cooler. The internal furnace was banked.

Petra shook the water out of her hair, shielding the basket from the spray, and stepped out into the night.

Wispwater in the evening was heavy and soft. Smoke triggered the memory of hunger. The air was thick with it—woodsmoke from a hundred hearths, weaving together with the damp, earthy smell of the dying bracken.

She walked to the inn, bypassing the noisy front taproom for the kitchen door around the back.

At her knock, Marda opened the door instantly,

releasing a cloud of steam that smelled of roasted root vegetables and sage.

"Petra," Marda said. "Late."

"Done," Petra said. She handed over the empty basket.

Marda took it and handed back a heavy, fresh one. "Lamb stew. Extra roll. You look like you've shrunk."

"I haven't shrunk, Marda. I'm just tired."

Petra took the new basket. It was warm. Quickly, surreptitiously, while Marda glanced toward the noisy taproom, Petra reached into the old basket, grabbed the wrapped mug, and slid it into the new one, right next to the hot crock of stew.

"Eat it while it's hot, smith," Marda said, turning back to her stove. "The iron will be there in the morning."

The door clicked shut.

Petra walked back through the village, clutching the basket to her chest. It was a warm counterweight to the chill. The street was mostly empty now. She watched the squares of yellow light in the windows—families eating, arguing, living.

When she reached her cottage, she didn't go inside. She walked around the side, boots crunching on the frost-hardened grass, to the back porch.

It was her sanctuary. A small wooden deck facing the dark slope of the mountain.

Petra sat in her rocking chair. It groaned under her weight.

She unpacked the basket. She set the stew on the small table. She took out the green mug and placed it on the railing. It sat there, dark and glossy in the moonlight.

She ate slowly. The stew tasted of earth and comfort —rosemary, carrots, tender lamb. It was fuel.

Then—

Strum.

Petra froze, the bread halfway to her mouth.

The sound drifted over the stone wall. A single, clear chord.

She melted farther back into the shadows.

Strum. Pluck. Hum.

Emil was on his porch. She saw the golden spill of his lantern light stretching across the frost-tipped grass. She saw the shadow of his hand moving against the side of his house.

He was playing.

It wasn't a lesson song. It was something wandering. A melody that climbed up the scale, faltered, and tried again.

The Secret Ritual.

Petra closed her eyes. The music was cooler than the pump water. It washed over her, finding the places where the noise of the forge was still ringing in her ears. It loosened the tight cables of her neck.

Pluck. Strum.

"C-sharp," she whispered.

She ate in the dark, accompanied by the serenade of the man she couldn't bring herself to talk to.

The melody shifted. It became faster, a run of liquid

notes like rain on a tin roof. It was beautiful. It was lonely.

Then, abruptly, it stopped.

Silence rushed back in.

Petra opened her eyes. She saw the shadow of his hand still hovering. He was sitting there, facing the wall. Facing her.

He tilted his head.

Petra held her breath.

Emil sighed. It was a soft sound. He stood up. His chair scraped.

He didn't speak. He just picked up his lantern. The light retreated, shrinking until the door clicked shut. The lock slid home.

Petra let out a long breath. She slumped back in her chair.

She looked at the green mug on the railing.

It wasn't doing any good here. It was a tool. Tools needed to be used.

Petra stood up. She wiped her hands on her trousers. She picked up the mug.

Before she could talk herself out of it, she stepped off her porch. The grass was stiff with frost. She walked to the low stone wall that separated their yards. It was waist-high, built of loose slate.

The schoolteacher's house was dark now, save for a faint glow from an upstairs window.

Petra swung her legs over the wall. She moved silently—surprising for her size, but she knew where the ground was hard. She crept across his yard, feeling like an intruder, a giant in a garden of gnomes.

She reached his back porch.

She didn't go up the steps. She just reached over the railing and set the wrapped mug on the small table beside his empty chair.

As she set it down, it made a tiny clink.

Petra flinched. She froze, staring at the back door.

Nothing happened.

She turned and ran—a lumbering, silent run back to the wall, vaulting it with a grunt of effort, and landing back in her own safety.

She sat back in her rocking chair, her heart hammering against her ribs like a trapped bird. She stared at the dark shape of his house.

"Goodnight," she whispered.

3

Petra woke before the bell.

This was wrong. Her body usually clung to sleep like a barnacle to a hull, fighting the tide of the morning until the very last second. But today, her eyes snapped open while the room was still grey.

Her heart was doing a frantic, skipping rhythm against her ribs.

The mug.

The memory of the night before—the frost on the grass, the silent creep across the yard, the tiny clink of ceramic on wood—rushed back. It felt foolish in the cold light of day. It felt huge.

She kicked off the blankets. The cold air was a slap, but she didn't armor herself immediately. Instead, she padded across the floorboards in her shift, shivering, to the small window in her kitchen.

It looked out on her back garden, the short wall, the back garden of the teacher's home, the porch.

She stood to the side of the frame, pressing her back against the cold plaster, and peered around the edge of the curtain.

Emil's porch was empty. The green mug sat on the table exactly where she had left it, a dark spot against the morning frost.

Petra waited. Her breath fogged the glass; she wiped it with her sleeve.

A moment later, the back door opened.

Emil stepped out.

Tall and rangy, he unfolded from the doorway like a carpenter's rule. Straw-blond hair, a messy halo in the damp air, and his long limbs seemed to get tangled in the thick wool cardigan he'd buttoned wrong at the collar. Even from here, Petra could see the width of his mouth and the roundness of his eyes—features that always made him look perpetually surprised, or delighted, or both.

He was holding a small ceramic bowl in his long fingers, steam rising from it. Tea in a bowl? Because he broke his mug.

He blinked at the morning brightness, shivering just as she was.

He turned to the small table.

He stopped.

Petra held her breath.

Emil stared at the mug. He reached out, tentative, as if

checking if it was a hallucination. He touched the green glaze.

Then, he picked it up. He turned it over in his hands, examining the curve, the handle, the weight. It was a good mug. Fen's work always felt like it belonged in your hand, like it had been waiting for you.

Emil looked up.

He didn't look at the sky. He didn't look at the garden. He looked straight at the stone wall. Straight at her shimmering, frost-covered cottage.

A smile broke across his face. It wasn't the polite smile he gave the parents. It wasn't the patient smile he gave the children. It was a soft, private thing. A sunrise.

He lifted the mug slightly, a silent toast to the invisible neighbor.

Petra ducked back behind the wall, her face burning. She slid down the plaster until she was sitting on the floor, knees pulled to her chest.

She shouldn't have done it. It was too intimate.

It was just a mug. A replacement tool.

But she knew, as she sat there shivering on the floorboards, that it wasn't just a tool. It was a sentence. And she had just started a conversation she wasn't sure she could finish.

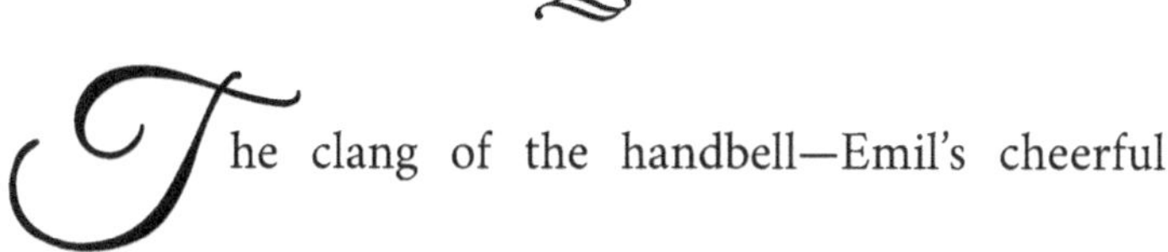

The clang of the handbell—Emil's cheerful

morning summons—finally sounded, releasing Petra from her kitchen.

She dressed quickly. The layers felt less like armor today and more like... clothes. Just clothes.

She walked the path to the forge, and when she passed the library railing she usually checked, she barely glanced at it.

Lightness. It was a dangerous feeling for an Anchor. Anchors needed weight to hold the line. If she floated, who would keep the valley safe?

But the air felt crisp, and the woodsmoke smelled sweet, and she couldn't quite suppress the memory of that smile.

She reached the smithy. The fire woke easily today, the coals catching on the first strike.

By mid-morning, the forge was roaring. Petra was working on a set of fire-irons for the inn—twisting the heavy square-stock while it was orange-hot, spiraling the metal like ribbon.

Strike. Twist. Strike.

The rhythm was good.

The big double doors of the forge were open to let out the heat. From her anvil, if she stepped just to the right, she had a clear view down the sloping road back toward the village center. She could see the slate roof of the schoolhouse and the green patch of the yard.

She heard the children first—the shrill chaos of recess. Then the handbell calling them to order.

Then she saw the visitor.

Linnea Valerius was walking up the path from the village. The tea shop owner looked like a wind-blown flower in her layers of scarves and knitwear, carrying a basket with the distinct purpose of a woman on a mission.

Petra wiped her forehead with her wrist.

Linnea didn't turn to come to the smithy. She turned up, toward the schoolyard.

Petra moved closer to the shadow of the doorway, watching.

She saw Linnea approach Emil, who was seated on a bench tuning his lute while the children ate their lunch. Linnea set her basket down. She poured something from a thermos—steam rising in the cold air.

Service. Care. Linnea was the valley's heart, pumping warmth to the extremities.

Emil took the cup. He said something that made Linnea laugh—a sound that Petra could've sworn drifted faintly up the hill.

Then, Linnea turned. She pointed.

She pointed right up the hill. Right at the open door of the forge.

Petra froze. She felt exposed, even in the dark.

Emil looked where Linnea pointed. He gazed up the road. Even at this distance, Petra felt the weight of that look. It wasn't a casual glance. It was a search.

Linnea said something else. She touched Emil's arm—a gentle, encouraging pat—and picked up her basket.

She walked out of the schoolyard. And she kept walking. Down and up the street, up the hill. Toward the smithy.

Petra scrambled back to the anvil. She grabbed the fire-poker she had been twisting. It was cold now, black and dull. She shoved it into the coals anyway.

"Petra?"

Linnea's voice was light, chiming over the roar of the bellows.

Petra turned, feigning surprise. "Linnea."

The other woman stood in the threshold. She didn't enter—the heat was too much for her delicate constitution—but she leaned in, her cheeks flushed from the climb.

"I brought you a bun," Linnea said, holding out a paper-wrapped parcel. "Lenore said you missed breakfast."

Petra took it. Big, warm, cinnamon and yeast. "Thank you."

Linnea didn't leave. She stood there, wrapping her scarf tighter, her eyes sparkling with that knowing look. Once an Oracle, always an Oracle, apparently.

"I had tea with Emil," Linnea said casually.

"Oh?" Petra kept her face still. Stone.

"He has a new mug," Linnea noted. "A beautiful one. Pine green."

"Fen makes good pots," Petra said.

"He said it appeared on his porch this morning," Linnea said. "Like magic. He thinks it was the moss gnomes."

"Gnomes are notoriously clumsy," Petra grunted. "They would have broken it."

Linnea smiled. It was a terrifyingly gentle smile. "He likes it, Petra. He likes it very much."

She turned to go, pausing just as the wind caught her hair.

"The tea leaves were interesting this morning," she added, her voice dropping to that floaty, distant tone she used when the sight touched her. "They showed iron singing. I've never heard iron sing before."

Petra blinked. "Um, sure?"

Linnea smiled, and the moment passed. "Eat the bun, Petra. You need the strength."

She drifted back down the hill.

Petra stood there, the warm pastry in one hand, the cooling tongs in the other.

Iron singing?

She looked at the poker in the fire. It was glowing cherry red.

She pulled it out and struck it.

Brrring.

It wasn't a thud. It was a clear, high bell-tone that echoed in the rafters.

Petra stared at it.

It seemed the forge was having a good day too.

4

The lightness lasted until five o'clock.

It was a good run. For Petra, four hours of feeling like she wasn't bolted to the floor was a record. She finished the fire-irons for the inn. She repaired a harrow for the southern farm. She even hummed—a low, rusty sound that got lost in the roar of the bellows—as she worked.

She thought about the green mug. About the way Emil's face had broken into that sunrise smile.

The man could drink tea from a bowl. She struck a rivet, shaking her head. Ridiculous. Creative.

The door banged open.

Jonas, Marda's little stable boy, stumbled into the forge. Tall already at twelve, he'd gone pale under his freckles.

"Smith," he gasped, hands on his knees. "The cart. In the square."

Petra lowered her hammer. The lightness evaporated instantly, replaced by the familiar tug of gravity. "Whose cart?"

"Ferdie's. The mail cart. It just... sat down. Like a donkey."

"Did he hit a rut?"

"No," Jonas said, eyes wide. "He was just rolling. And then, crack."

Petra didn't ask anything else. She didn't take off her apron. She grabbed her heavy leather tool belt—the one with the pry-bars and the emergency clamps—and strode out the door. The lightness was gone. The anchor was back on duty.

~

The village square was usually the fulcrum of Wispwater's bubbling tranquility. An ancient oak tree in the center, a stone well, the benches where the elders sat to complain about the weather.

Today, it was a scene of wreckage.

Ferdie's bright red mail cart, the most reliable vehicle in the valley, was listing dangerously to the left. It looked like a bird with a broken wing. Mail was spilled across the cobblestones—letters, parcels, and bundles of newspapers scattered like fall leaves.

At least there was no wind.

Ferdie stood in the middle of it, wringing his red felt

hat in his hands. He looked unhurt, but bewildered. His white beard bristled with distress.

"I didn't hit anything, Petra," he said as she approached. "I swear it. Smooth stones. I was just turning the corner toward the bakery and—" He made a crushing motion with his hands.

A small crowd had gathered. Marda was there, directing some children to pick up the mail. Sam from the general store watched with folded arms.

The miller, Thom, knelt by the broken wheel. A big man, broad-shouldered in a way that came from lifting flour sacks rather than hammering steel, he looked up as Petra arrived. His face was grim.

"Here," Thom said, pointing to a piece of the wheel.

Petra bent down, looking at the wheel.

The iron rim—a continuous band of steel she had forged herself—hadn't just bent. It hadn't slipped off the wood.

It had snapped.

A clean, jagged break at the six o'clock position. The metal had sprung outward, shattering the wooden spokes and collapsing the hub.

"That's a two-inch band," Petra said, her voice flat. "It doesn't just snap. It bends, at least a little. It squeals. Iron warns you."

"Not this time," Thom said.

Petra knelt beside him. The cobblestones were cold against her knees. She reached out and touched the jagged edge of the iron tire.

It felt wrong.

Usually, when iron broke—which was vanishingly rare—the edge was sharp and bright, screaming with the violence of the separation.

This edge was dull. Gray. It looked… porous.

Petra rubbed her thumb against the fractured metal.

It crumbled.

A fine gray dust coated her skin. Almost ash. Grit.

She froze. She looked at Thom.

"Rot?" she whispered.

Structural failure at the molecular level. The grain structure was gone.

"I forged this," Petra said. She stood up, wiping the gray dust onto her apron, but the stain didn't leave her skin. "I forged this just two years ago. Three. I quenched it in oil. I tempered it to straw-yellow. It was perfect."

"I believe you," Thom said, standing up to join her. He had that ash over the flour on his hands. He must have just made a delivery. "But now?" He shrugged, a giant move on his broad shoulders. "It's hollow."

Ferdie fluttered over to them. A small man, light enough to be carried off by a stiff breeze, with bright, sparrow-like eyes and a white beard that seemed to defy gravity. "Can you fix it, Petra? I have a delivery for the Sutter Farm. It needs to arrive today."

Petra looked at the wreckage. She looked at the gray dust on her thumb.

If it was a bend, she could heat it and straighten it. If it was a crack, she could weld it.

But this? This was the metal giving up.

"I can't fix this rim, Ferdie," she said. Her voice sounded heavy, loud in the quiet square. "I have to forge a new one."

"Today?" Ferdie asked, hopeful.

"It will take me until sundown," Petra said. "If I start now."

"Start, then," Marda called from the pile of letters. "The mail doesn't wait, and neither does the frost."

Petra turned to go back to the forge.

"Petra," Thom said quietly.

She stopped.

Thom was holding a piece of the shattered iron spoke. He crushed it in his hand, and it turned to powder, drifting away on the wind.

"That's not wear and tear," he said, his voice low enough that Marda couldn't hear. "Iron doesn't forget how to be iron."

But it did. Sometimes. Never for her, but for others. She'd heard stories, whispered among the fellows during city guild meetings.

Had it come for her? For Wispwater?

She turned and walked back up the hill. The lightness of the morning was a distant memory now. Her boots felt twice as heavy as they had an hour ago.

Around her, the valley looked the same—the great oak, the warm homes, the trees, the schoolhouse roof.

But when she reached the forge, the fire in the hearth looked different. It wasn't welcoming. Petra opened her hand and let the gray dust drift into the coals. It didn't spark. It didn't hiss. It just vanished, silent and cold, into the heat.

5

The inn was usually the warmest place in the valley. It smelled of bread and roasting meat, of damp wool and spilled ale. It sounded like laughter.

Tonight, it sounded like worry.

The tables had been pushed back to the edges of the taproom, leaving a rough circle of floorboards in the center. Marda stood by the hearth, her arms crossed, looking less like an innkeeper and more like a general reviewing troops before a siege.

Petra stood near the door.

She liked the door. It was an exit strategy. It was also the coldest spot in the room, where the draft seeped in under the oak jamb, and right now, she needed the cold. Her skin still felt prickly, as if the gray dust from the rim was stuck in her pores.

The room was full.

Ferdie was there, looking shaken, clutching a mug of

cider he wasn't drinking. Elder Garrett from the southern farm sat on a stool, nursing a bandaged hand. Several of the weavers, the tanner, and the glazier were clustered by the bar.

The village's beloved baker, the effervescent Lenore, sat near the fire, shivering. She an Thom were newly wed. She leaned back against him as he stood, a solid wall of presence.

And Emil. Her neighbor.

He sat on a low bench near the musicians' corner, his long legs folded up awkwardly. Sam Jenka sat beside him, talking with her hands, probably about what songs she'd learned lately. Sam could hold a tune like no one else in the valley.

"Alright," Marda said. Her voice carried through the murmurs without effort. "Let's have it out. Garrett?"

The farmer stood up slow. Getting on in years, with no children to take over the farm, he just kept working. He held up his bandaged hand.

"It was the hoe," he said, his voice trembling—not just with indignation, but with something that sounded like betrayal. "I turned the winter beds. Just turned them! And the blade didn't just bend on a rock. It shattered. A piece flew up and cut me."

He pointed a gnarled finger at Petra. "I've used that hoe for ten years, smith. We trusted you. We trusted your iron. But now this. And it keeps happening."

Petra didn't flinch. This was the job. When the iron

held, the village thrived. When it broke, the smith answered.

"I forged a replacement," Petra said, her voice steady. "Is it working for you now?"

"It's fine," Garrett grumbled

"And will that one shatter too?" someone shouted from the back. The tanner. "My fleshing knife snapped this morning. Clean in two. I gave you the benefit of the doubt on the first one, Petra. But twice?"

"And the gate hinge at the school," Emil added.

The room erupted into a low buzz of complaints. Everyone had a story. A nail that crumbled. A pot hook that gave way. A horseshoe that disintegrated.

They were scared. Petra could smell it. Sour and sharp, cutting through the ale. Wispwater relied on iron. Iron held the roofs up. It held the wheels on. It held the tools together. If the iron failed, the valley stopped.

"It's the batch," Petra said loudly, stepping forward. "I must have gotten a bad shipment of ore. It happens. The carbon content is off. It's brittle."

It was a lie. She knew it was a lie. But it was a manageable lie. It was a problem with a receipt, not a problem with the universe.

"I'll re-forge everything," she continued, looking around the room. "Bring me the broken tools. I'll strip them down and re-mix the metal. I'll work through the night if I have to."

"You're one woman, Petra," Marda said, not unkindly. "There are fifty farms."

"I can do it," Petra said. "I'm the anchor."

"You look tired," Lenore said softy from the fireside. "Petra, you look exhausted."

"I'm fine," Petra snapped.

"She's not fine," a voice said.

The room went quiet.

Emil unfolded himself from the bench. He stood up. He was taller than most of the farmers, though he usually stooped to hide it. Tonight, he was standing straight.

He walked to the center of the circle. He looked at Garrett. He looked at the tanner. Finally, he looked at Petra.

"It's not her skill," Emil said. His voice was calm, the voice he used when breaking up a playground fight. "And I don't think it's the ore."

"What do you know about iron, teacher?" Garrett grumbled.

"Nothing," Emil admitted. "But I know about resonance. And I know about exhaustion."

He picked up the fire-poker from the hearth—one Petra had made years ago. He held it up.

"Petra is the best smith in three valleys," he said. "If she says she quenched it right, she quenched it right. If she says the temper was true, it was true."

He turned to the room.

"You're asking her to fix the unfixable. You're asking her to hold up a building where the bricks are turning to sand."

"So what is it then?" Marda asked, eyes narrowing.

"It's the Rust," Emil said.

The word hung in the air.

"It's a sickness," he continued, gaining confidence. "My gran told me stories from the old country about it. Weakness, not in the metal, but… in the connection. The iron is lonely. It's forgotten its purpose."

"Lonely iron?" The tanner scoffed. "Stick to poetry, teacher."

"Laugh if you want," Emil said, and there was a sudden flash of steel in his soft voice. "But look at the dust on your boots, Tanner. That isn't just rust. That isn't oxidation. That's despair."

He looked toward the door. Toward Petra, his dark eyes wide and serious.

"You can't anchor dust, Petra," he said. "You can't hammer a powder back into a solid. You need… something else."

"What else?" Petra asked. She felt stripped bare. He had seen right through her 'bad batch' lie. He had seen the terror underneath.

"I don't know," Emil said. "But I know you can't do it alone."

He looked around the room. "We don't need to pile more work on the smith. We need to figure out why the valley is losing its grip."

Silence stretched out.

Then Thom stood up. The miller walked over to Petra. He placed a heavy hand on her shoulder.

"He's right," Thom said. "Structurally speaking. The

material integrity is compromised. Re-forging won't help if the physics has changed."

Ferdie leapt to his feet. "The council—we have records," he said. "Old books. About the founding of the valley. Maybe there's something in there about a special rust."

Marda looked at them—the smith, the teacher, the miller, the messenger. The core of the valley.

She sighed. She uncrossed her arms.

"Fine," Marda said. "No more accusations. Bring the broken tools to the forge, but don't expect miracles by morning. Petra, you sleep tonight. That's an order."

The tension broke. The meeting dissolved into small, worried clusters of conversation.

Petra stood frozen by the door. She felt light-headed. She had prepared herself for anger. She had prepared herself for extra work.

She hadn't prepared herself for someone to defend her.

Emil walked toward the door, toward Petra. He paused as he passed her. He didn't stop, and he didn't touch her, but he leaned in close enough that she could smell the old paper and lavender soap scent of him.

"I liked the mug," he whispered.

Then he was gone, slipping out into the night.

6

The forge at midnight was usually Petra's favorite place.

Alone in the night, a world of specific, controllable physics. Heat radiating from the banked coals. The smell of cooling oil, iron dust. Shadows jumping against the walls when she pumped the bellows. In the dark, the village disappeared, the world disappeared. There was only the metal and the will to shape it.

But tonight, the physics were broken. And Petra was breaking with it.

Petra stood at the anvil, staring at the hoe blade she had just forged.

It looked right. The curve was true, the edge beveled. The iron had taken on that lovely matte blue-gray of cooling metal.

She had folded it three times. She had done it the way she always did. But the metal felt… silent.

Fresh iron hummed. It held the memory of the fire for hours, radiating a low-frequency warmth that Petra could feel in her teeth. This blade was cold. It defined "object" in a way that made her skin crawl. It was just a thing. A shape.

"Talk to me," she whispered.

The blade didn't answer.

She moved the blade to the slack tub. The water hissed—a short, angry sound—and then fell silent.

She wiped her forehead with the back of her wrist. Soot smeared across her skin, mixing with sweat. She'd been working for hours. Since the meeting ended. She had three hoes, a gate hinge, and a pile of nails to show for it.

They all felt dead.

It must be exhaustion. She'd worn herself out. The metal was fine.

It had to be fine.

She grabbed the tongs, her hands shaking. She plunged the iron back into the pure white heat of the anthracite. The sparks flew up, biting at her arms, but she didn't feel them.

One more time. Just one more time. Keep the heat. Hold the song.

What if it really was her? What if she'd lost her link to the soft magic of the valley?

But she'd been a smith for twenty years. She'd apprenticed three towns over, and done a couple years in the city. She'd been a fine smith everywhere she'd ever worked.

And she'd never lost her link before. She'd never heard of such a thing.

Even the strangers, like Linnea, who came from the city, could feel the magic of the valley.

Had it deserted Petra?

Panic, cold and sharp as a filed edge, twisted in her gut. She hammered harder, the rhythm frantic, breathless. Clang. Clang. Clang. Not music. Noise. She was drowning out the silence with noise.

The knock at the door was so quiet she almost missed it.

It wasn't the heavy pound of a farmer needing a shoe, or the sharp rap of Marda delivering an order. A hesitant, rhythmic tap, just a one-two-three.

Petra froze. For a moment, she considered pretending she didn't hear it. Use the hammer. Keep working. If you stop, the silence comes back.

The door creaked open a few inches.

"Petra?"

Emil.

Her heart hammered against her ribs. A different rhythm, erratic and terrified. He couldn't be here. He couldn't see this.

"No," she croaked. "Go away."

He shouldn't be here. The forge was the edge of town. It was late. He was a teacher, and teachers needed sleep, and neighbors didn't visit neighbors at midnight unless their house was on fire.

"I saw the light," he said, slipping through the gap.

He brought the cold in with him—a draft of crisp autumn air that swirled the coal dust on the floor. He wore a heavy wool coat with black metal buttons over his clothes, and a thick blue scarf wrapped twice around his neck. In his hands, he held a covered jug.

"You're working," he said. It wasn't a question. He looked at the pile of finished tools, then at her face.

"I need to," Petra said. Her voice came out rusty. She realized she hadn't spoken since the Council meeting. She stepped in front of the anvil, trying to block his view of the failed hoe. "The hoe. The hinge."

"Marda said sleep."

"Marda isn't the smith."

Emil closed the door behind him. He didn't retreat. He walked further into the room, into the circle of heat thrown by the forge. He looked so out of place here. Too tall, too clean, too soft for the hard angles of the anvil and the vise.

But he didn't look afraid.

"I brought cider," he said, lifting the jug. "Spiced. Ideally, it helps with sleep. But you can also use it for fuel."

He set the jug on the workbench, clearing a space among the rasps and calipers with careful fingers.

"You defended me," Petra said. She hadn't meant to say it. It just fell out.

Why had he done it? They were neighbors, sure, but in the 'wave from the porch' kind of way. He'd never singled her out before. He'd never stepped between her and a jagged edge like Marda or the Council.

Until today.

Emil paused. He kept his eyes on the jug as he unstoppered it. "I stated facts. You can't fix what isn't broken."

"You said the iron was lonely."

"Is it?"

He turned to look at her. His dark eyes seemed lighter in the firelight, and very serious.

Petra looked at the hoe blade in the slack tub. She looked at the anvil, the hammer, the tongs.

"It's quiet," she admitted. "It usually… sings. When I hit it. A ring that lasts for seconds. Tonight, it's just a thud."

"Lack of resonance," Emil said. "The connection is dampening."

He reached into his coat pocket and pulled out two mugs. Not bowls. Mugs. One was chipped blue ceramic. The other was the green mug.

Petra stared at it.

"I washed it," Emil said, pouring the steaming cider. "And I thought… well. Iron needs fuel, so the smith needs cider."

He held it out to her.

Petra took her forge gloves off. Her hands were slick, calloused and scarred. His were long, pale, soft. When his fingers brushed against hers, the contact sent a jolt through her.

"Thank you," she said, startled.

"You're welcome, neighbor."

He picked up the blue mug and leaned back against the workbench, looking around the shop. "I've never been in here at night. It's..."

"Dirty?"

"Alive," he said. "It feels like the inside of a heart. Hot. rhythmic."

He reached out toward the pile of new nails on the cooling rack.

"Don't touch those," Petra warned. "They're still—"

"Hot?" Emil hovered his hand over them. "No. They're cold."

He picked one up. A four-inch spike, forged an hour ago.

Petra stepped forward. "It can't be. I finished that batch... it hasn't been long enough."

She reached for another nail.

As her fingers grazed the metal, the nail didn't just feel cold. It felt wrong.

Emil gasped. Petra's gaze snapped to his hand.

The nail Emil was holding disintegrated.

It didn't break in half. It crumbled. One moment it was a steel spike; the next, it was a handful of gray grit pouring through his fingers like sand.

Emil looked at her. "Did I do that?" he asked, eyes wide.

He turned his hand over, dusting the powder off his coat.

Petra stared at the pile of gray dust on the floor.

"No," she whispered. The cold from the door seemed to rush back in, settling deep in her bones. "I did."

She turned to the hoe blade in the slack tub. She grabbed it with her bare hand—reckless, stupid, but she had to know.

It wasn't hot. It wasn't warm.

She squeezed.

The steel crunched. Faster than dry clay. Chunks of expensive imported iron dissolved, sprinkling gray dust into the water.

"It's not just the old iron," Petra said, and her voice trembled. "It's the new iron too."

Emil set his mug down. He looked at the dust on the floor, then at Petra.

"The Rust," he said softly.

The Rust? He'd called it that at the meeting. "What do you know about it?" she asked. The words came out sharper than she'd intended.

"Not much," he said. "Just Gran's stories, from across the sea."

Then how did it get here?

Petra looked at her hands. "I can't be a smith if the metal won't hold. I'm just… a person playing with dirt."

Emil stepped closer. He reached out and took her hands—dust, soot, and all—in his.

"Then we find out why," he said.

"How?"

"I'll search for that reference," he said. "And I'll write to a librarian in the capital for more."

"And me?"

"And we, we'll listen. To the metals, to the fire. Tomorrow. Tonight... you sleep."

He squeezed her hands, then let go. He picked up the green mug she had set down and placed it gently back in her hands.

"Drink the cider, Petra. The iron will wait. But you need to rest."

He walked to the door. "Goodnight, neighbor."

"Goodnight," Petra whispered.

The door clicked shut.

Petra stood alone in the silence of the forge. He was right. She needed to rest, to give her mind time to mull over the problem.

The crisis.

In the forge, the fire was still hot. But everything else —the anvil, the racks, the tools—felt terrifyingly cold.

7

The Town Hall records room didn't smell like fear. It smelled like dry paper, binding glue, and the bergamot sachets Linnea insisted on tucking into the shelves to "clear the stagnant energy."

"I still can't believe Marda gave us the key," Petra said.

She stood near the doorway, staying clear of the narrow aisle. The room was really just a glorified walk-in closet behind the Council chambers, lined floor-to-ceiling with wooden shelves that sagged under the weight of Wispwater's history. Town ledgers. Birth records. Crop yields from fifty years ago.

"She wants answers," Emil said. He leaned back against a shelf, crossing his long legs at the ankles. He took up too much space in the small room, but unlike Petra, he didn't seem to mind. He looked comfortable in the squeeze of books. "And she knows I'm the only one bored enough to read the tax codes from the Year 340."

Petra shifted her weight. Seeing him so at ease made her feel even stiffer, like a poorly-oiled hinge.

"He's in his element," Linnea said from the table. "Ignore him."

Emil was indeed in his element. In the classroom, he sometimes struggled to rein in the energy of two dozen children. But here, among the ghosts of old writers, he moved with a fluid, terrifying competence. He pulled a volume from a high shelf, blew the dust off the spine—a gentle puff, like blowing out a candle—and opened it without creaking the binding.

"Sit, sit," he said to Petra. "Plenty for all of us to look through."

Linnea was already at the reading table, a long flat oak slab that used to be the council table before the council decided to sit in a circle. All manner of books were stacked beside her—some bound in leather, some in paper, some in bark.

The tea shop owner always looked like she had just drifted in from a different reality. Linnea wore three layers of shawls, all in different shades of moss and lavender, but Petra noticed that underneath the soft wool, her posture was rigid. She sat with the straight back of a woman who had once navigated the Royal Court, not just a tea counter. She smelled of dried sage and expensive city soap—comfort covering a core of steel.

"Got it," she said. "The founding charter." Her soft voice carried a weird, vibrating weight. The "Oracle voice" she tried to hide behind tea and cookies. "And the original survey maps. Did you know the river used to run closer to the eastern ridge?"

"Hydrology is fascinating," Emil said, setting a book next to Petra, starting a pile for her. "But we need metallurgy. Or theology. Or whatever passes for magic in a ledger."

Petra sat down heavily. Her boots felt too heavy on the wooden floor. In the forge, she knew where every hammer hung. She knew the temper of every pair of tongs. Here, she was useless. She couldn't hammer a sentence into shape. She couldn't heat-treat a paragraph to make it stronger.

"What am I looking for?" she asked.

Emil looked up over the rim of his spectacles. She'd never seen him wear reading glasses before. They made his eyes look bigger, like a cat's.

"Patterns," he said. "The Rust can't be new. If it happened across the sea, it might have happened here too, a long time ago. Look for gaps in the records. Look for years where the tool orders spiked, or where the harvest failed because the plows broke."

Petra nodded. "Look for broken things," she said. That, she could do.

She pulled a ledger from the nearest shelf. *Year 342 - Smithy Inventory.*

She opened it. The handwriting was cramped and spiky, fading to brown.

Three gross nails. Two plowshares. One axle, reinforced.

Normal. Boring.

She flipped forward a decade. *Year 352*

Four gross nails. Three scythes. One gate mechanism for the miller.

She worked for an hour. The silence in the room was heavy, broken only by the rustle of turning pages and the scratching of Emil's pen. It made Petra's skin itch. She wanted the roar of the bellows. She wanted the ring of the anvil. Silence, to her, meant the fire had gone out.

"This is useless," she muttered, slamming a ledger shut. "It's just lists. Nails and horseshoes and hinges. It tells us what. It doesn't tell us why."

"Wait," Linnea said.

She wasn't looking at a ledger. She was holding a thin, cloth-bound book with the reverence most people saved for babies. Her fingers, tanned and smooth, hovered over the page without touching the ink.

"Listen to this," Linnea said. "It's from the journal of Mathias, a First Elder. He's talking about the building of the first bridge."

She cleared her throat. "The stone holds. The timber holds. But the iron refuses. We forged the heavy bolts three times, and three times they snapped in the cold night. The metal is stubborn. It does not know us yet."

She didn't read like a schoolteacher. She read like she was remembering the words.

"He personifies it," Emil said thoughtfully. "Usually, you'd say the metal is 'brittle' or 'impure,' right? He calls it 'stubborn.'"

"Is there more?" Petra asked. She leaned across the table toward Linnea.

Linnea traced the next line. "We called for the Anchor. She did not bring a hammer. She brought a song. She sat with the iron for three days and three nights. She told it where it was. She told it what it needed to be. And on the fourth day, the bolts held."

A chill ran down Petra's spine. "The anchor," she repeated. "That's… that's a title. Marda calls me that. She says, 'You're the anchor of the valley.'"

"I thought it was a metaphor," Emil said. "Like 'pillar of the community.'"

"So did I," Petra whispered.

She looked at her hands. The callouses, the burns, the scars. Evidence of hard work. Of physical force. She had spent twenty years beating metal into submission, forcing it to take the shape she wanted.

She did not bring a hammer.

No hammer? What did that even mean?

But the idea of singing… Petra did do that, sometimes. She hummed while she worked. She hummed while she hammered. She hummed while she forged. A slow, raspy sort of tune made the bellows of the forge sing. Short, fast notes could make the metal sing.

"It's a special song?" she asked. "But I do sing, sort of." She leaned back in her chair. "I hum, all the time. And I haven't changed my methods. I haven't changed my tools." She frowned. "But the metal has changed."

Emil sat beside her, concern in his overlarge eyes. "You're sure? Nothing has changed?"

Petra nodded. And then gasped.

"Have I been doing it wrong?" she asked. The realization hit her harder than a kick from a nervous horse. "All this time. I thought the job was to be strong. To be the hardest thing in the room."

"Maybe it is," Emil said. He took the book from Linnea and looked at the faded ink. "But maybe 'hard' doesn't mean 'rigid'. Maybe it means 'resonant'."

"Resonant?" Petra repeated. "Like a bell?"

Emil was watching her like she was a bug. A very interesting bug. "Like a bell," he said.

"Mathias calls it a song," Emil said, tapping the page. "But functionally? It's a tether. A line of communication. You're the connection point, Petra. You're the one who introduces the iron to the valley."

He looked at her, his voice dropping. "If you stop talking to it..."

"...it gets lonely," Petra whispered.

The word stuck in her throat.

She had been working double shifts for weeks. She went from the forge to her bed and back again. She hadn't had dinner with Lenore in a month. She hadn't listened to Emil play music in the evenings. She had filled the silence with hammering, with noise, but she hadn't connected with anything. Not the iron. Not the people.

"And it leaves," she finished.

It fit. It fit perfectly with the crumbling nail, the silent anvil, the cold dread in her stomach. The metal wasn't breaking because it was weak. It was breaking because of her. Because she was disconnected.

"So how do we fix it?" Linnea asked. She looked from Emil to Petra, her green eyes wide. "Do you need to... sing to it? Or sing more? Sing differently?"

Petra laughed, a short, sharp bark of sound. "I don't sing. Especially not to hoe blades."

"You hum, you said." Emil frowned. "But I didn't hear you humming when I came to see you this afternoon."

Petra froze. "What?"

"That's right," Linnea said. "You weren't humming when I came by, either."

Petra's face flushed. "I've been so busy." The humming was just a way to keep her mind from wandering. A way to focus on the task at hand.

"I've been tired," she said, crossing her arms defensively. "I've been working nonstop to fix everything. And redo the new pieces that weren't coming out right."

"And in the rush," Emil said, tapping his chin, thinking, "you stopped the conversation."

He tapped the book again.

"So. We have a theory," he said. "The Rust is a failure of connection. The hypothesis is that re-establishing the tether will fix it."

Petra grabbed the edge of the table, needing something solid to hold onto. Could it be that easy?

"So I just go back to the forge, hum a little tune, and all the broken iron magically fixes itself?"

"Hypothetically," Emil said. "But it's not that simple." He looked at Linnea as if for confirmation. "Whatever this is... it's advanced. The connection is already severed. We can't just repair it. We have to..." He gestured with his hands, a weaving motion.

"Re-weave it," Linnea said. Her face lit up as if she'd won a prize. "How clever."

Then her face fell. "But, how?"

"Something loud," Emil said, thinking out loud. "Something powerful."

"We need a ritual," Linnea said, nodding. "Something that wakes the iron up. The valley listens to intent, Petra. You know that."

What sort of ritual could wake up metal? Petra had no idea.

"Maybe I can just talk to it, but louder," she said. "More. Would that work?"

Emil shook his head. "I don't know." He smiled, taking the sting out of the words. "But it's worth a try."

"Tomorrow," Petra said. "Tomorrow, I'll try. I'll take the deepest breath I've ever taken, and I'll... I don't know. I'll talk to it."

Linnea reached across the table and took one of Petra's hands. Hers smelled of tea and chamomile. "And we'll help you."

Emil put his hand on Linnea's. "And I'll keep looking

for more details. There might be a particular frequency. Or a pattern."

Petra looked at the shelves of books. Thousands of books. Millions of words. And in the end, the answer wasn't in any of them. The answer was—maybe—in a song she didn't even know she was singing.

8

Petra unlocked the heavy iron padlock, her breath pluming in the cold morning air. She pulled on the door, and the gray light of dawn spilled across the shop floor, cutting a path through the darkness to the foot of the anvil.

The air inside was still and cold, scented with ash and iron. Entering the forge was like walking into a warm embrace. Today, it felt like walking into a crypt.

Before she could step inside, she paused. She took a deep breath, trying to clear her head. She closed her eyes and tried to hear the sound of the Great Anvil ring in her ears.

Instead, she heard footsteps approaching.

"We're early," Emil said from behind her. Sunday, so no school today. He shifted his weight on the gravel, shivering slightly in his coat. He had brought his notebook, a fresh pen, and a thermos of coffee. He looked like a mad scientist preparing to observe a volatile chemical reaction.

"The valley wakes up with the sun," Linnea said. She drifted past them, carrying a basket covered in a linen cloth. "Transitions are powerful. Dawn is the best time to start something new."

Or end something old.

She walked to the center of the shop. To the great anvil.

A massive block of iron, the anvil was anchored to a stump of petrified oak that went deep into the earth. It had been here since the founding of the town. Its surface smoothed by generations of hammers.

The heart of the forge. The heart of her life.

She stepped to the forge, to wake up the coals. Then she turned to Linnea.

"What do I do?" Petra asked. Her voice sounded too loud in the quiet room.

"Set the stage," Linnea said. She began pulling things from her basket. A beeswax candle, which she lit and placed on the corner of the workbench against the anvil. A bundle of dried sage, which she didn't light, but crumbled into a small ceramic bowl. "We're not casting a spell, Petra. We're creating a space where the iron knows it's being listened to."

"I'm listening," Petra said. She pressed her palm onto the cold face of the anvil. "I'm always listening."

"But are you responding?" Emil asked. He leaned against the table, pen already moving, sketching the scene. "Remember the journal. Magic here is a conversation."

Linnea looked up at him. "Sometimes."

Petra took a deep breath. She reached for her hammer—her favorite one, the three-pound cross-peen with the hickory handle that had molded to her grip over twenty years.

It felt heavy today. Heavier than usual.

"Just… hum?" Petra asked.

"Start with the hum," Emil said. "Find the resonance. Then, when you feel it… strike."

Petra closed her eyes.

She tried to find the place in her chest where the hum lived. Usually, it came naturally. It came when she was thinking about the angle of a bevel or the heat of a rivet. Now, with Emil watching, with Linnea burning candles, it felt forced.

She felt ridiculous. A grown woman, a seasoned smith, humming at a block of metal like a child talking to a doll.

No, she told herself. Not a doll. A partner.

She forced a sound out. A low, vibrating note deep in her throat.

It sounded flat. Weak.

"Louder," Linnea whispered. "Mean it, Petra."

Petra thought about the crumbling nail. She thought about the hoe blade snapping like a twig. She thought about the fear in Marda's eyes, the accusation in the farmer's voice.

Told herself: I am the anchor. I hold the line.

She pushed the sound deeper. She let it rattle in her chest.

She felt a vibration. Not in the air, but in her hands. The hammer seemed to wake up. The anvil seemed to… wait.

"That's it," Linnea said softly.

"The frequency is shifting," Emil agreed. "Like a tuning fork."

Petra felt the heat of embarrassment rise in her face. But she also felt a connection. A thin, wavering, fragile thread reaching out from her to the iron. It was there.

It was still there.

She wasn't broken.

She raised the hammer.

She let the hum build, a crescendo of intent. *I am here. You are here. We are together.*

She swung.

She listened for the ring.

The Great Anvil was famous for it. A clear, bell-like tone that could be heard from the village hall to the grist mill. The sound of order, of strength, of safety.

The hammer connected.

Thud.

The sound was sickening. No bell. Not even the satisfying clang of metal on metal. More like the dull, wet smack of a hand hitting a bag of sand.

No shockwave rang out. Instead the force of the blow

traveled straight up the handle, jarring Petra's bones, rattling her teeth.

The hammer bounced, dead in her hand.

Petra stumbled back, dropping the tool. It hit the floor with a clatter. A normal clatter, a normal sound.

Silence rushed into the room. Absolute, heavy silence.

"Did I miss?" Petra whispered. She stared at the anvil.

There was a dent in the face. A dent. In hardened steel. "I... I dented it."

Linnea put a hand over her mouth. The candle flame on the bench flickered and went out, though there was no breeze.

Emil walked slowly to the anvil. He reached out and touched the surface.

"It absorbed it," he said. His voice calm, purely observant, though his hand shook. "It took the energy and... swallowed it."

"It didn't ring," Petra said stupidly. A chill claimed her. Colder than she had ever felt in her life. "It didn't answer."

Linnea shivered. "Petra... Is the spirit gone?"

Petra grabbed the hammer from the floor. "No. No, I just... I didn't hit it right. I didn't hum loud enough."

She swung again. Wildly. Without rhythm.

Thud.

Thud.

Thud.

Each blow a funeral bell. Dull. Broken. Lifeless.

Emil grabbed her arm. "Petra, stop!"

"It works!" Petra shouted, struggling against him. "It has to work! I'm the smith! If I can't wake it up, who can?"

"Not now!" Emil shouted back. He wrestled the hammer from her grip and threw it into the corner.

Petra collapsed against the anvil. She pressed her forehead against the cold, dead metal. "Gone," she said. "It's all gone."

She waited for the echo. For twenty years, every strike had an echo. But there was nothing. Just the blank, flat silence of a world where physics had won and magic had lost.

Without the echo, who was she? Just a woman in a dirty apron. Just a person hitting things with a stick. The anchor wasn't real. The tether wasn't real. She was alone in a cold room with two people who were realizing, right now, that she was a fraud.

Linnea came to her side, wrapping one of her own shawls around Petra's shoulders. Petra shivered. Linnea's touch was warm.

"It's not gone," she said. "It's just… quiet."

The silence in the forge was absolute. Outside, the world seemed to have stopped too. No birds sang. The wind didn't rustle the leaves. Wispwater held its breath.

Emil paced, from the anvil to the door. Back to the anvil. Tapping his notebook against his hand. He opened it, looked at it blindly, closed it again.

Tilted his head. Listening.

"It's not just gone," he said quietly.

He turned his head, cocking it to the side, like a bird listening for a worm.

"The silence," he said. "It's not empty. It's... heavy."

"Heavy?" Linnea asked. She moved to stand beside Petra, wrapping one of her shawls around the smith's shaking shoulders.

"It's like a room where the conversation just stopped," Emil said. He walked to the window, but he didn't look out at the mountains. He looked at his own reflection in the dusty glass. "The potential is there. But the language is wrong."

He turned back to them. His face was pale, but his eyes were sharp.

"We can't force it," he said. "You proved that, Petra. Hammers won't work. The iron has stopped listening to force."

Petra looked up. Swallowed. Pushed the panic down. "Then what's left? If I can't hammer it, I can't shape it."

"Physics," Emil said, a strange, small smile touching his lips. "If a frequency is cancelled out, you don't shout louder. You change the pitch."

He looked at his hands—long, slender, made for plucking strings, not bending steel.

"We need to teach the iron a new song."

9

Petra was sweeping.

Monday. The fire should be roaring, the bellows singing, and the schedule for the week chalked onto the slate by the door.

Today, the slate was blank. The fire was cold.

Petra pushed the broom across the stone floor, gathering the gray dust into a pile. It was fine as flour, soft and slippery. It was supposed to be a hoe blade. It was supposed to be a gate latch. Now, it was just dirt.

She was a person playing with dirt.

She stopped. She leaned on the broom handle, staring at the pile.

The morning light filtered in through the windows, cold and unforgiving. It illuminated the silent shop. The anvil sat in the back of the room like a tombstone, the dark forge the hole in the ground waiting for the body.

She should close the shop. Put a sign on the door: Closed for Repairs. Or better: Closed for Lack of Soul.

But she couldn't. Habit was a strong tether, even when the anchor was gone. She had woken when Emil rang the school bell. She had dressed in her heavy wools. She had walked to the forge.

She just didn't know what to do next.

The door opened.

Petra didn't look up. "We're closed, Ferdie. I can't fix the cart."

"It's not Ferdie."

Petra flinched. She looked up.

Emil stood in the doorway. He wasn't wearing his usual school clothes; no tweed jacket, no practical shirt. He wore a thick fisherman's sweater and heavy trousers tucked into boots. And on his back, strapped tight with leather bands, was a black instrument case.

"You're not at school," Petra said.

"I gave them homework and left Marda's eldest in charge," Emil said. "Teacher's holiday." He walked in, closing the door behind him. He looked around the silent, cold shop. He looked at the pile of gray dust. "Research day."

He walked to the workbench and swung the case off his back. He set it down on the only clear space, right next to the vise.

"What are you doing?" Petra asked, voice flat. She felt too brittle for conversation.

"We have a theory," Emil said, unbuckling the case. "We need to test it."

"The theory is broken, Emil. The iron is dead."

"The iron is silent," Emil said. He opened the case. Inside, nestled in blue velvet, was his lute. The wood was polished to a honey glow, the neck inlaid with mother-of-pearl. It looked ridiculously fragile in the heavy, industrial space of the forge. "There's a difference."

He picked it up. He plucked a string. The sound was bright, sharp. Annoying.

"Don't," Petra stuck out a hand. "Please. It's... it's like laughing at a funeral."

Emil looked at her. His face was serious, but kind. Too kind. "I'm not laughing, Petra. I'm working."

He pulled a wooden stool—the one Marda sat on when she came to complain—over to the anvil. He sat down. He adjusted the instrument on his knee.

"You said you hummed," he said. "For twenty years, you hummed intent into the metal. A low frequency. A vibration."

Petra gripped the broom handle. "A hum. Not a song. It was... part of the work. Like breathing."

"Exactly," Emil said. "It was subconscious. Innate. But now, the connection is severed. The iron can't hear you anymore. Or maybe..." he struck a chord, a sadder tone that hung in the air, "...maybe it's just deaf to that specific frequency."

He looked at the anvil. "So we find a new one."

"You want to play music to a block of steel?" Petra

asked. "Emil, this is dangerous. If I strike it and it shatters... the shards are sharp. They could cut you. They could cut the lute."

"I trust you," Emil said.

"You shouldn't." She gripped the handle tighter, her knuckles white. He didn't know what a misfire could do. She had seen a splinter fly right through a leather apron once.

Emil ignored that. "Pick up your hammer."

Petra didn't move. She just wanted him to leave before something broke. Before something broke him.

"Petra," he said, his voice firm. Teacher voice. "Pick up the hammer."

Petra let out a breath—a ragged, defeated sound. She leaned the broom against the wall. She walked to the anvil. She picked up the cross-peen. It felt heavy. Dead weight.

This was a bad idea.

"Ready?" Emil asked.

He began to play.

It wasn't a song. It was a scale. Up and down. Precise. Mathematical. Do-Re-Mi-Fa-Sol...

"Strike," he ordered.

Petra tapped the anvil.

Thud.

The dull sound swallowed the music.

Emil frowned. He adjusted a peg on the lute's neck. "Again."

He played a different scale. Lower. Slower.

Petra struck.

Thud.

"Again."

He tried a faster tempo. A jig.

Thud.

"Again."

A waltz.

Thud.

Half an hour passed. The forge remained cold. Petra's arm ached, not from exertion, but from the impact of the dead metal. Every strike jarred her shoulder. Every thud was an insult.

"Emil, stop," she said, dropping the hammer onto the bench. "It's not working. You can't math your way into magic."

Emil stopped playing. He sat there, staring at the strings. His hair stuck up in tufts where he'd run his hands through it. "The physics should work," he muttered. "Resonance is resonance. Sound waves are physical force."

"Maybe the iron doesn't care about physics," Petra said. She leaned against the anvil, crossing her arms. "Maybe it just... knows I'm a fraud."

Emil looked up. "What? You're not a fraud."

"I am. I've lost my grip. Smiths don't break iron. They heal it."

She looked at him. He looked so out of place here. So soft. And yet, he was the only one trying.

"Why are you doing this?" she asked. "You're a

teacher. You have a warm classroom. You have tea with Linnea. Why are you sitting in a freezing forge playing scales to a rock?"

Emil rested his hand on the strings to silence them. He looked at her. Really looked at her.

"Because I drift," he said.

Petra waited, still.

"I live in my head, Petra. In books. In theory. Half the time, I forget to eat until Linnea brings me a bun. I forget to sleep until the fire goes out."

He looked down at the lute case.

"I float away. But you… you are absolute. You are certain."

He looked up at her again.

"When I found that mug on the porch, it wasn't just a replacement for the one I broke. It was… weight. You saw I was drifting, and you handed me a rock to hold onto."

"It was a mug, Emil. Fen made it."

"It was gravity," he insisted. "You anchored me. You didn't just fix a tool. You fixed me."

He took a breath. "I don't want to live in a world where things just crumble, Petra. I need the weight. I need your weight."

He didn't wait for her to answer. He didn't check his tuning pegs. He just started playing.

It wasn't a scale. It wasn't a jig.

He played a slow, rambling melody. A wandering tune that climbed up, faltered, and tried again.

Petra froze.

It was the song from the porch. The song he played at night, just before turning in for bed.

That beautiful, rambling song that had become the soundtrack to her nights.

He played it softer this time. Intimate. The notes rippled through the fire-tinged air of the forge, bouncing off the stone walls, finding the corners where the shadows lived.

It wasn't perfect. It was a little lonely. A little longing.

Petra's chest went tight. She closed her eyes. She could see the frost on the grass. She could see the lantern light.

She reached for the hammer.

She didn't think about it. She didn't calculate. She just let the music pull her hand.

The melody swelled—a rising phrase, hopeful and terrified.

Petra swung.

Hummmmm.

It wasn't a ring. It wasn't the sharp, bell-like clang from before.

It was deeper. Richer.

A sound like a cello bowing a low C. A vibration that didn't just travel through the air, it traveled through the floorboards. Through the soles of Petra's boots, up her legs, into her lungs. Into her heart.

The anvil vibrated under the hammer.

Emil's eyes went wide. He didn't stop playing. He

leaned into it, matching the pitch of the hum, weaving his notes around the resonance of the iron.

Petra struck again. And again.

She wasn't hammering the metal. She was playing the anvil.

The sound filled the room. Warm, alive. It pushed the cold back into the corners. It wrapped around them—the smith and the bard—binding them together in a chord of iron and wood.

The pile of gray dust on the floor shifted, just slightly, in the vibration.

Emil finished the phrase with a long, sustained note.

Petra let the hammer rest on the face of the anvil. The hum slowly faded, drifting into silence. But it wasn't the dead silence of before. More like a moment of rest.

Emil lowered the lute. His hands shook.

"That," he whispered, his voice breathless. "That wasn't physics."

Petra looked at the anvil. She touched the face of it. It was warm.

"No," she said. She looked at Emil. "That was jazz."

Emil laughed. A sudden, startled sound that broke the tension completely.

"Jazz," he repeated. "The smith plays jazz."

He stood up, slinging the lute strap over his shoulder. He walked over to the anvil. He didn't touch it. He just stood close to her.

"It worked," he said.

"It worked," Petra agreed. She looked at her hammer. "But Emil..."

"Yeah?"

"I can't do that alone," she said. "I can't hum that. It needs the strings. It needs... the counterpoint."

Emil nodded. He understood.

"Then I guess I have a new job," he said. "Afternoon shift?"

Petra looked at the slate board by the door. The blank schedule.

She walked over to it. She picked up the chalk.

Monday: 4 PM - Rehearsal.

She turned back to him.

"Bring tea," she said.

Emil smiled. The sunrise smile.

"Deal."

10

If the first attempt was jazz, the second was a train wreck.

And the third, a dirge.

"No," Petra said, lowering her hammer. "You're dragging."

"I'm keeping a steady four-four time," Emil argued. He was perched on her taller stool, a wobbly confection of metals leftover from other projects. His brow furrowed in concentration, the lute cradled against his chest like a shield. "You're the one speeding up. On the upswing."

"Because metal cools, Emil! I can't wait for the down-beat if the iron is already turning gray."

She shoved the cooling nail into the slack tub. It hissed—a short, angry sound—and she tossed it onto the pile of failures. The twelfth. Twelve bent, brittle, useless nails.

"We need a faster tempo," she said, wiping sweat from her forehead. "A jig. Something with drive."

"A jig is too bouncy," Emil countered. "If I play a jig, you'll start hitting in triplets, and we'll end up with a corkscrew."

They had been at this for three days already. The miracle of Monday afternoon had turned into the slog of Tuesday, Wednesday, and Thursday.

It turned out that magic, like everything else, required technique. Practice. Patience. And a willingness to look like a fool.

"Let's take a break," Emil said. He set the lute down in its case, treating it with reverence. He flexed his fingers, and then blew on the tips. At Petra's raised eyebrow, he said, "Lute strings are unforgiving. I'm not used to playing for four hours straight."

Petra leaned a hip against the anvil. The metal was warm beneath her good leather apron. Her shoulder throbbed in time with the crackle of the fire.

"We don't have time for breaks. Ferdie needs these by noon."

"Ferdie needs nails that won't disintegrate." He reached for the water jug, poured two cups, and handed one to her.

Petra took it. Her hand brushed his. His skin was cool; hers was burning hot.

"It shouldn't be this hard," she muttered. She drank the water in one long gulp, and then sighed. "Ideally, we just... resonate."

"Ideally, I don't have blisters," Emil said, looking at his left hand. "And ideally, you don't look like you're trying to murder the anvil."

He stood up and stretched, up and up. His palms almost touched the ceiling. He walked over to her. The forge wasn't that big, designed for one large person and hot metal, not one large person, hot metal, and a long-limbed teacher with a fragile instrument. He was in her space. The forge shouldn't smell so of rosin and paper and... man.

"You're tight," he hovered a hand near her shoulder. "You're bracing for the impact before you even swing."

"Because I'm expecting a thud," Petra admitted. She rolled her shoulder, trying to loosen the knot of tension there. "My body remembers the shock."

He reached out and touched her arm, just above the elbow. "If you're rigid, the vibration stops at your shoulder. It needs to go all the way through you."

"I can feel it get caught, right there," she said.

"Can you listen past it?" he asked. "Don't wait for the hammer, wait for the string?"

His touch was light, clinical. A teacher adjusting a student's grip. But in the heat of the forge, with the door closed against the winter chill, it felt... loud.

Petra pulled her arm back. "I know how to hold a hammer, Emil."

"And I know how to hold a rhythm," he said, not backing down. "We're both professionals. But we're playing a duet neither of us knows the music for."

He went back to the stool. He didn't pick up the lute. He just sat there, watching her.

His gaze was quiet, but it had weight. It felt like another tool in the room—calipers, maybe—measuring her patience. Petra shifted her weight, resisting the urge to wipe the soot from her cheek. She hit the anvil with the hammer, a light tap just to fill the silence.

"What?" she asked.

"Talk to me," he said. "Not about tempo. About the nail. What does it need?"

Petra looked at the bar of stock in the fire. "It needs to carry weight," she said. "It needs to bite into the wood and hold. It needs to be stubborn."

"Stubborn," Emil repeated. He nodded. "Okay."

He picked up the lute. He didn't play a scale. He played a chord—a low, dissonant, grinding sound. It made her wince.

"Like that?" he asked.

Petra frowned. "Maybe?"

Emil took the sound into another key or something, a deeper groan. This time, the chord resolved, slowly, into clarity. It sounded like a heel digging into dirt.

Petra felt the vibration in her teeth. "Yes. At the end."

"So this time, don't strike on the beat," Emil said. "Strike on the resolution. Wait for the tension to break."

He played the chord again. Brrr... ping.

Petra pulled the iron from the fire. It was glowing orange-white.

Brrr...

She held the hammer raised, her muscles trembling with the urge to swing.

...

She struck.

HUM.

The sound was short, sharp, and resonant. The nail flattened perfectly under the blow.

Brrr... ping.

HUM.

Brrr... ping.

HUM.

They fell into it. It wasn't a song you could dance to. More like a conversation. The lute asked a question—complicated, tense—and the hammer answered it—simple, definitive.

The pile of good nails began to grow.

The air in the forge changed. It grew lighter, charged with the strange harmony of gut-strings and steel. Petra stopped thinking about her shoulder. She stopped thinking about the schedule. She just listened for the resolution.

She didn't hear the door open.

She didn't know anyone was there until the song ended on Emil's long sigh, when a slow, dry clapping cut through the air.

Petra spun around, hammer raised.

Fen stood in the doorway. The potter had scrubbed

the gray clay from their skin, their broad shoulders filling the frame in a clean wool sweater. They had eyes the color of slate and a presence that felt less like a person entering a room and more like a mountain settling into place.

Petra lowered the hammer.

Emil stood up quickly, nearly knocking over the stool. "We were just... experimenting."

Fen walked into the already stuffed room. They moved with the slow, deliberate gravity of a glacier. They ignored Emil. They ignored Petra. They walked straight to the cooling rack.

They picked up one of the new nails.

Petra held her breath. If Fen frowned... if Fen looked at it with those slate-gray eyes and saw emptiness...

Fen ran a thumb over the head of the nail. They tapped it against the rack.

Tink.

Clear. Bright. Alive.

Fen looked at Petra. Their face, usually as readable as a stone wall, cracked into a tiny, almost invisible smile.

"Loud," Fen said.

"Too loud?" Emil asked anxiously.

Fen shook their head no. "Clear."

They looked at the lute. Then at the hammer.

"Clay likes song too," Fen said. "I sing to the wheel. Low. It helps the walls rise."

Emil blinked. "You do?"

They put the nail back.

"Good batch," Fen said.

They set a heavy ceramic mug on the workbench—one of the special ones, glazed in deep forest green. A match to Emil's own. It smelled of spiced cider and steam.

"From Linnea," Fen said.

They turned and walked out, their boots leaving no trace on the soot-stained floor.

Petra let out a breath she felt like she'd been holding for an hour. She looked at Emil. Who was grinning.

"Iron likes conversation," he repeated. "See? I told you."

"You told me to wait for the resolution," Petra corrected, though she couldn't help smiling back. "Different thing."

"Same thing," Emil said. "Resolution is just the end of the argument."

She checked her pocket watch. "Three o'clock. We have the nails. Ferdie will be happy."

He sighed. "Do more today?"

"Maybe," Petra said. "Maybe not."

He started to pick up the lute. His movements were slow. His shoulders slumped. The energy of the performance was fading, leaving the exhaustion behind.

"You're tired," Petra said.

"I'm wrecked," Emil admitted. "Teaching twenty kids all morning and then wrestling physics for three hours? I'm going to sleep for a week."

"You have class tomorrow," Petra reminded him.

"Don't remind me." He latched the case. "Reviewing multiplication tables while hearing that hum in my head... it's distracting."

"You're still hearing it, too?" Petra asked.

He looked at her. "Does it stop? The vibration?"

Petra felt her own hands. They were still buzzing. A low-level current that ran up her arms. "No," she said softly. "I don't think so."

"Good," Emil said. He swung the case onto his back. "Same time tomorrow?"

"We have hinges to do," Petra said. "Hinges need a waltz."

Emil laughed. "I'll practice my three-four time."

He opened the door. The winter light spilled in, harsh against the warm glow of the coals.

"Petra?" he said, pausing.

"Yeah?"

"We're good at this," he said. "The duet."

Petra looked at the pile of perfect nails. She looked at the teacher, with his worn-through fingers and his grand imagination.

"We're adequate," she said, gruffly. But the gruffness had no heat in it. "Go eat a sandwich, bard."

"Yes, smith."

He left.

Petra stayed in the quiet forge. She picked up one of the nails. It was still warm. She held it to her ear.

If she listened closely, she could almost hear the ghost of the chord. Brrr... ping.

She put it in her pocket. Ballast.

She wasn't just a person playing with dirt anymore. She was a person playing music.

And for the first time in weeks, the anchor felt solid.

11

The Week of the Singing Nail, as it would later be known, ended with a scream.

Not a human scream. A horse scream.

Petra was in the back of the forge, sorting through a bucket of scrap metal, when she heard it. It was a high, terrified whinny that cut through the winter air like a knife. Then came the sound of hooves skidding on ice, the groan of wood, and a man shouting.

"Hold! Easy! *Easy,* Buster!"

Petra dropped the scrap bucket and ran for the door. Emil, who had been sitting on her stool retuning the G-string for the tenth time, was right behind her.

They burst out onto the cobblestones.

The temperature had dropped sharp and sudden that morning, turning the damp square into a sheet of black glass.

Ferdie's delivery cart was jackknifed at the corner of

the square. One wheel was up on the curb. The horse, a massive dappled gelding named Buster, was rearing, his eyes wide and rolling with panic.

"His hoof!" Ferdie yelled, hanging onto the bridle with both hands. "He's thrown a shoe and the hoof is splitting!"

Petra didn't hesitate. She ran towards the horse. Horses in pain were dangerous—half a ton of muscle governed by pure fear—but Petra had been shoeing Buster since he was a foal.

"Buster, hey," she said, her voice dropping into the low, rumbling register she used for frightened animals. "Hey, big man."

She moved around the thrashing animal, keeping close to the shoulder where the hooves couldn't reach him. She crouched down.

"Left foreleg!" she said. "Shoe is gone. Hoof wall cracked right up to the coronet band. He can't put weight on it."

"We have to get him off the ice," Ferdie said. "Get him into the forge."

It took ten minutes of coaxing, shoving, and terrified sweating from all three of them—Petra, Ferdie, and Emil—to get Buster into the stall next to the side door of the forge. The moment the horse's hooves hit the dirt floor, with the lean-to roof over his head, he settled slightly, though he still trembled, holding the injured leg high.

The lean-to—and the forge front door—were wide open. A crowd was gathering. Marda from the inn, Thom from the mill, a gaggle of kids with nothing better to do since their teacher was on forge duty. They stood just outside the threshold, a wall of curious, frightened faces.

Petra examined the hoof. It was bad. The cold had made the keratin brittle, and the skid on the ice had sheared off a chunk of the wall.

"I can't nail a standard shoe onto this," she said, wiping her hands on her apron. "There's nothing to anchor it to. I need a bar-shoe to bridge the crack, and I need to shape it to the break."

But then she looked through the side door, at the simmering forge. At the unpredictable anvil.

Panic spiked in her chest.

"I can't forge it," she whispered. "If I strike it, it's just going to be dead weight. It won't hold the vibration of the road. It will shatter the first time he trots."

Ferdie looked at her, his face pale, imploring. "Petra, he's in pain. If he can't walk..."

He didn't finish the sentence. A draft horse who couldn't walk was a tragedy.

Petra looked at Emil.

He had gone inside, and was standing by the work-bench, his hand resting on the neck of his lute. He wasn't looking at the crowd. He was looking at her.

"We can do it," he said.

Petra shivered. She stepped into the smithy. "In front of everyone?" she whispered. "If we fail... if the shoe shatters... it's cruel."

"Then don't fail," Emil said. He picked up the lute. He

didn't ask permission. He walked over to the tall stool and perched on it.

The crowd murmured.

"Is teacher going to play a lullaby?" a young voice chirped.

"Is he crazy?" said someone in a lower register.

"Petra," Marda called out from the door, her voice sharp. "This is an emergency, not a recital. Do you need me to get the stunning hammer?"

Petra looked at Marda, her face lined with concern. At Buster, who was sweating and blowing hard. At Emil, who was ready and waiting for her.

"No," Petra said. Her voice shook, just a little. "We're good."

She walked to the coal bin. She shoveled fuel into the forge. She worked the bellows until the fire roared, orange and hungry. She thrust a bar of stock into the heart of the heat.

"Emil," she said, keeping her back to the door. "If you make me look stupid, I'm going to weld your tuner to your nose."

"Understood," Emil said. "What's the rhythm?"

Petra watched the metal heat. She pictured Buster's hoof, the repair, the shape she needed to make. She thought of the rhythm of her hammer, the rhythm of the forge. She asked the iron.

"It's a heartbeat," she said. "Heavy. Fast. But steady."

"Got it."

Emil began to play.

He started with a percussive slap on the body of the lute, mimicking the heavy pulse of a large animal. Then he added the notes. Low, driving, insistent.

It sounded like a gallop in slow motion.

The crowd went silent. Even with the forge roaring, his music was loud in the small space, amplified by the stone walls.

Petra pulled the glowing iron from the fire.

She put it on the anvil.

She waited.

Thump-thump. Strum.

She swung.

HUM.

The sound rang out into the square. It wasn't the dead thud of the last week. It was the rich, cello-growl they had found in practice.

The crowd gasped.

Petra didn't look at them. She looked at the iron. It was moving under her hammer like clay, soft and willing. She bent it into a circle. She drew out the clips. She punched the nail holes.

Thump-thump. HUM.

Thump-thump. HUM.

Emil picked up the tempo. The heart beat faster. Petra swung faster. They locked into the groove—the same sweat-soaked, desperate focus they had found yesterday.

Buster lowered his head. His ears swiveled toward the music. The trembling in his flank stopped.

"Hold the leg," Petra ordered Ferdie.

She grabbed the shoe with her tongs. It was cooling to a dull cherry red. Emil started to lift his hands from the strings.

"No," she said. "Don't stop. Play it... play it into the hoof."

"What?"

"The vibration," Petra said. "It soothes him."

Emil nodded. He softened the volume, shifting from a gallop to a trot. A gentle, loping melody.

Petra lifted Buster's leg. She placed the hot shoe against the hoof. Smoke billowed up, scented by burnt hair, but the horse didn't flinch. He was listening to the lute.

Petra drove the first nail.

Tink.

True.

Second nail.

Tink.

Third nail.

She worked around the hoof, clinching the nails, rasping the edges. The bar-shoe bridged the crack perfectly, shifting the weight to the frog and saving the wall.

She set the hoof down. It had already cooled enough in the chilly air that she didn't have to worry about it.

"Walk him," she told Ferdie.

Ferdie looked at her, then at the horse. He clicked his tongue. "Come on, Buster."

The horse took a step. Then another. He put his weight on the left foreleg.

He didn't limp.

The clip-clop of the shoe on the stone road was clear as a bell.

Ferdie let out a whoop. He threw his arms around the horse's neck. "You beauty! Petra, you didn't just fix it, you… you sang it!"

Petra wiped the sweat from her face. She leaned against the smithy wall, her knees suddenly feeling like water.

"Petra?" Emil asked, his voice soft.

She looked toward him. And then past him, to the open doorway.

The crowd was staring at them. Mouths open.

Marda stepped forward. The formidable innkeeper looked at the horse, then at the shoe, then at the lute in Emil's lap.

"Well," Marda said. Her voice carried, like always, over the crowd. "I suppose that's one way to skin a cat. Or shoe a horse."

She nodded to Emil. "I didn't know you had it in you, schoolmaster."

Emil stood up. He looked exhausted, he looked exultant. He bowed with theatrical flourish. "It's all physics, Marda."

"Physics," Marda snorted. "Right. And my stew causes hallucinations."

She walked over to Petra.

"The Festival of Frost is Saturday," Marda said. "We usually have the fiddlers from the ridge."

Petra stiffened. "Marda, no. We're not a band."

"Of course not," Marda said. "You're the people who just saved the mail cart with a guitar. You'll be our guests of honor. First round is on the house."

She turned to the crowd. "Show's over! Unless you want to pay them for an encore, clear out!"

The crowd dispersed, chattering excitedly. The word magic floated back on the wind.

Petra slid down to sit on the ground. She put her head in her hands.

"Guests of honor," she groaned.

Emil sat down next to her. He bumped her shoulder with his.

"Free drinks, smith," he said.

Petra looked at him through her fingers. He was grinning, that wide, sunny smile that made her chest wobble.

"You are impossible," she muttered, though she didn't pull her hands away.

"I'm essential," Emil corrected. "And you need my weight."

Petra sighed. Down the street, Ferdie was leading Buster in a victory lap.

"Yeah," she admitted, soft enough that the iron couldn't hear. "I guess I do."

12

Petra stood in front of the small, pitted mirror in her bedroom, staring at a stranger.

The woman in the glass was not the blacksmith. The blacksmith was made of wool and denim, soot and sweat. She had edges. She had utility.

This woman was… soft.

The dress was a deep, forest green velvet. The color of moss found on the north side of a tree. It caught the candlelight and swallowed it, shimmering with a plush, dangerous depth. One of Marda's daughters had sewn it, and Marda had insisted on the color. "It matches your eyes, you stubborn mule," she'd told Petra.

Linnea had done something complicated with Petra's hair, pinning the heavy strands up with combs so that her neck was exposed.

Petra touched her throat. It felt naked. Without her

high collar, without her leather apron, she felt like she'd lost her shell. Vulnerable to the air, to eyes, to judgment.

"You look ridiculous," she told the reflection.

The reflection didn't argue. It just looked back, wide-eyed and terrified.

She turned away from the mirror. She paced the small room in the impractical, too-soft shoes. The velvet swished around her legs with an angel's whisper that grated on her nerves. She needed weight. She needed ballast.

She stopped at her dresser. She pushed aside the jar of arnica cream and the tin of boot polish until her fingers brushed against cold metal.

The First Nail.

It was rough, unpolished, and perfect. She picked it up. The bite of the iron against her palm was instant relief. A tether to reality. To her world.

She slipped the nail into the hidden pocket of the dress. The heavy fabric sagged just the slightest bit on that side.

Center of gravity restored.

She grabbed her heavy wool cloak and stepped out into the biting winter night.

~

The inn wasn't just loud. It was vibrating.

The sound hit Petra half a block away, a thumping, scraping, laughing roar that promised heat and chaos. Condensation frosted the windows, turning them into glowing squares of amber against the dark snow.

She hesitated at the bottom of the wide wooden steps that led up to the inn's front porch. The party smelled of roast goose, caramelized onions, pine needles, and the sharp, coppery tang of mulled wine. A good smell, a Wispwater smell, but tonight it made her stomach turn over.

Usually, she'd slip in through the kitchen, nod to Marda, and find a dark corner to nurse a stout until the noise became too much. But tonight, she was a "Guest of Honor." Guests of honor didn't use the kitchen door.

The front door swung open before she could reach for the iron handle.

Emil stood there, framed by the golden light of the taproom.

He wasn't wearing his tweed. No ink-stained cuffs. He wore a waistcoat embroidered with silver thread that matched the frost on the railings, and a cravat of dark blue silk. He belonged on a stage.

His smile shifted. The quick, amused grin slowed, turning wondering.

"You're late, smith," he said, but his voice was soft.

"I was considering fixing the church gate instead," Petra admitted, clutching her cloak tighter. So many people were here. "It squeaks."

"The gate will wait." He stepped out onto the porch, the cold air seemingly unable to touch him. He offered her his arm. "The goose is carved, and Marda has threatened to use the stunning hammer on anyone who touches the best pieces before you arrive."

He was solid. Steady.

She uncurled her hand from her cloak and looped it through his elbow. The silk of his sleeve was cool, but the arm beneath it radiated warmth.

"I feel like a parade float," she muttered as he led her toward the light.

Emil's laugh broke the tension in her chest. He leaned close, his breath brushing her ear. "You look," he whispered, "like the queen of the winter court. Terrifying and magnificent."

He opened the door, and the world exploded into sensory overload.

First, a wall of warmth that carried the scents of roast goose, spiced cider, and fancy people. Marda had gone overboard. Garlands of fresh pine hung from every rafter, tied with red ribbons. Candles flickered in jars on every surface, doubling the light, making the shadows jump and dance.

"There they are!" Marda bellowed from behind the bar. She was wearing a crown of holly that had slipped jauntily over one ear. She raised a tankard the size of a bucket. "The Iron Duet!"

The room erupted. Cheers, clapping, the stomping of boots.

Petra flinched. Instinct screamed at her to back up, to find a wall, to hide.

Emil didn't let her retreat. He didn't pull her forward, either. He just stood there, a solid presence at her side, grinning, absorbing the attention so she didn't have to take the full force of it.

"Smile and wave," he murmured. "Then we move to the edges."

He steered her expertly through the crush. So many faces, so many voices. A gauntlet of goodwill.

"Petra! My gate is holding perfect!" Elder Hemlock shouted, waving a tankard that was fortunately nearly empty.

"Saved my deliveries, you did!" Ferdie piped up, weaving through the forest of legs with the agility of a meadow mouse, a half-eaten meat pie held close to his chest.

They passed the large round table near the hearth.

Linnea sat close to the fire, laughing at something Fen said, snuggling the potter's arm. They were peeling a mandarin orange with focused, surgical precision, their large, clay-stained hands moving with impossible delicacy. As Petra passed, Fen looked up. They didn't smile, but they nodded—a slow, respectful dip of the chin.

It meant more than all the cheering.

At the next table, Thom the miller was sketching something on the back of some piece of paper for Lenore. The baker was leaning in, her face flushed from the heat of the ovens or the wine, watching his pen. She reached out and tucked a stray curl behind his ear, a gesture so casual and intimate it made Petra's chest ache. They were a unit. A closed circuit of affection.

She had no one. With Emil, though, she had a partner.

A physics partner.

"Secure location acquired," Emil announced, leading her to a small table tucked into an alcove between the fire and the window. It offered a view of the room but protected her back.

He disappeared into the fray and returned moments later with two mugs of cider, steaming and fragrant with cinnamon.

"You're good at that," Petra said, blowing on the steam.

"Crowd mechanics," Emil said, sliding into the seat opposite her. "Find the flow, interrupt the current, extract the prize." He clinked his mug against hers. "To not breaking anything."

"To structural integrity," Petra replied.

The cider was hot, sweet, and spiked with enough brandy to numb the panic in her knees. The room was chaotic, loud, messy, merry. For the first time in weeks, she didn't feel the crushing weight of the Silence. The Rust. The hum was here—not in the iron, but in the people.

The fiddlers on the dais finished a reel and struck up a slower tune. A waltz.

Emil set his mug down.

"May I?" he asked.

Petra stared at his open palm. Panic seized her chest,

tightening her lungs until she couldn't draw a breath. Longing surged up from her stomach, hot, warring with the icy instinct to flee. Her heart hammered. She wanted to take his hand. She was terrified to take his hand. Hope fluttered in her throat, tasting like copper.

"Emil," she managed, forcing the words past the knot of fear. "I don't dance. I maintain a stationary position. I am an anvil."

"Anvils ring if you strike them right," he said, his eyes dancing. "Come on. Three-four time. It's just geometry in motion."

Fen and Linnea had already moved into the dancing space. Linnea, in lace and laughter, easily found the rhythm. The potter, clad in the softest-looking blue wool tunic, followed her lead, their large hands steady on her waist.

"I have big feet," Petra warned. "I will cripple you."

"I'll risk it."

She put her hand in his. His fingers folded over hers, dry and warm.

He pulled her onto the floor.

She expected to feel clumsy. She expected to be the heavy, lumbering thing she always felt like in dreams. But Emil didn't try to drag her. He stepped into her space, put a hand on her waist lightly, respectfully, and waited.

She took a breath and stepped into the rhythm. He matched her step for step, his hand on her waist a steady anchor.

Emil was right; it wasn't magic. It was mechanics. He

created a vacuum, and she filled it. He shifted his weight, and she counter-balanced.

But it was kind of magic, too

"You're leading," she accused, breathless, as he spun her past the fireplace, the velvet of her dress flaring out like a bell.

"I'm merely suggesting direction," Emil said. He wasn't looking at his feet. He was looking at her. "You're providing the momentum."

"I'm heavy."

"You're solid." His hand tightened slightly on her waist. "You're real. Everyone else here… they float. But you?" He pulled her closer as they turned. "You're the ground."

Petra missed a step.

He caught her. He didn't let her stumble. He just adjusted the rhythm, turning the mistake into a hesitation step.

"I've got you," he whispered.

The room spun, but steadily. The pine, the candlelight, the faces. All of it blurred into a watercolor background. The only sharp thing in the world was the blue of his eyes and the pressure of his hand on her hand. Her back.

For a moment, just a heartbeat, Petra allowed herself to imagine it. Not the partnership. Not the work. But this. The two of them, spinning in the light, tethered not by necessity, but by choice. The thought was a spark that landed on dry tinder. Sudden, terrifying, impossible to stomp out.

Until the music ended.

They drifted to a stop near the back door. They were close. Too close. Petra could smell the soap on his collar, the faint tang of the cider. She could feel the heat radiating from him.

Her heart banged against her ribs like a trip-hammer.

"Air," Emil said, his voice a little ragged.

"Air," Petra agreed.

They stepped out onto the back porch.

The quiet of the winter night hit them like a soft slap. The snow had started to fall, thick, heavy flakes spiraling down through the lantern light like feathers.

Petra leaned against the porch railing, one hand gripping the cold wood. With the other, she reached into her pocket and touched the nail. Solid, warm from her body heat.

"We make a good team," Emil said to the snow. He stood next to her, looking out at the dark shapes of the mountains. In the dim light, he seemed less gangly. More settled.

"We do." His profile was a clean edge against the night —the messy hair, the tension in his jaw, the way he broadcast that hungry, desperate attention for life even when standing still. "I still think you're insane for bringing a lute into a forge."

Emil turned. He rested his hip against the railing.

"Insanity is repeating the same mistake and expecting different results. We tried something new."

He reached out. For a second, she thought he was going to touch her face. Instead, he brushed a snowflake from her shoulder. His hand lingered on the velvet.

"I'm glad you're my smith, Petra," he whispered.

Petra looked up at him. The snow was catching in his eyelashes. He looked soft. Open. Dangerous.

"I'm glad you're my bard," she whispered.

The space between them seemed to shrink. The air charged, heavy with the magnetic pull she had fought for years. The song of the porch was finally finding its resolution.

Emil leaned in.

Petra held her breath. She didn't pull away. She leaned forward, just a fraction—

A gust of wind slammed into the porch. Not a normal gust, but a sudden, biting chill. It swept across the porch, stripping away the warmth of the cider and the moment in a single breath. The lantern swung on its hook, casting wild, dancing shadows.

Above them, the heavy iron bracket holding the inn's sign groaned, a long, dissonant squeal of cold metal.

Petra flinched, the romantic haze shattering instantly. The blacksmith took over. She looked up at the bracket.

"That needs oil," she said, her voice sharp.

Emil squinted against the wind and looked up, through the snow, toward the sky. The clouds were churning. He shook his head and offered a wry, crooked smile.

"That's my cue," he said, stepping back and pulling his coat tighter against the sudden chill. "Tomorrow's almost here."

He gestured toward the door. "Go inside, smith. Before you turn into an ice sculpture. I'll see you tomorrow."

He didn't wait for an answer, but turned and headed down the steps into the snow.

13

Sunday morning came on a whiff of stale cider and the moaning of muscles unused to dancing.

Attributes of the morning included: a headache that throbbed behind Petra's left eye, a town square littered with pine needles, and a distinct lack of urgency.

Petra sat at the small round table in the window of The Steeping Kettle, nursing a mug of tea that Linnea promised would "realign her energies."

Petra didn't want her energies realigned. She wanted her headache to stop throbbing.

The shop was too clean, too neat. It reeked of lemon oil, dried lavender, and aggressive tranquility. The floorboards were scrubbed pale, and the the windows gleamed with a clarity that hurt Petra's eyes. Behind the counter, the tea canisters were arranged in a color spectrum unsettlingly precise. Light to dark. Floral to earthy.

An organizational system that made the chaotic pile of scrap metal in her forge look like a crime scene.

"You look," Emil said, peering at her over the rim of his own mug, "like you're trying to bend the spoon with your mind."

"I'm trying to figure out why this spoon is so light," Petra grumbled. She dropped the delicate silver utensil onto the saucer. It made a polite plink instead of a satisfying thud. "Everything in here feels breakable."

"That's the point," Linnea said, drifting over with a ceramic pot. She looked infuriatingly fresh—her hair braided in a crown, her dress crisp and smelling of rosemary. She poured more steam into Petra's cup. "It encourages mindfulness. Reminds us to be gentle, especially with ourselves."

"I am an anvil," Petra muttered. "I am not designed for gentle."

"You danced for hours last night," Emil pointed out. How could he be so chipper? He danced almost as long as she had, but his eyes were bright, his straw-blond curls only slightly less perfect than usual. "You have hidden depths of grace."

"I have blisters," Petra said. "And a headache that has its own pulse. How are you so... well?"

"Hydration," Emil said cheerfully. "And the moral superiority of the bardic arts."

Linnea smiled at Petra, a soft, terrifyingly understanding expression. "Drink the blend, Petra. It has willow bark and meadowsweet. It'll help."

Petra drank. It tasted like grass and wet stones, but the warmth did seep into her chest, loosening the knot of tension there.

Outside, the morning sun hit the cobblestones, turning the frost to slush. Across the street, the bakery was quiet, though the chimneys were puffing their usual white smoke.

"Do you think it stays?" Emil asked quietly, tracing the rim of his blue-grey mug.

"The snow?"

"The hum." He looked at the steam rising from his tea. "We proved it works on nails. On horseshoes. But does it stick? Or do we have to sing to every gate in town every week?"

"We'll find out," Petra said. "If Ferdie's horse starts limping on Tuesday, we know we have a shelf-life problem."

She was setting her cup down—carefully, so as not to crack the saucer—when the screaming started.

It came from directly across the street. Muffled by glass, but distinct.

"Help! Someone!"

Petra knocked the table as she stood up, rattling the china.

"Lenore," Linnea gasped.

Petra was out the door in a flash, Emil and Linnea not far behind.

Lenore burst out of the bakery, her face pale as flour. Usually, the baker moved with a birdlike, fidgety energy

—fast-talking and cheerful, a blur of dark hair and smiles. But today that energy had curdled into terror. She didn't look like the woman who brought extra scones to neighbors; she looked like someone escaping a fire.

"Petra!" she shrieked. "The oven! The big one!"

She grabbed Petra's arm with a grip that might leave a mark. "The upper hinge snapped. It's hanging by a thread, and bread is in there, and the heat... we can't shut it, and it's going to fall!"

They burst into the bakery.

The heat hit them like a hammer. Hotter than the forge, somehow; wet, yeasty, suffocating. The air was thick with smoke and the smell of burning sugar.

The scene was chaos. Behind the half-filled display counter, in the work area, trays of half-risen dough were scattered on the wide prep counter. Behind them, at the back of the room, the massive cast-iron door of the main oven was groaning.

The upper hinge had sheared cleanly off. The door, weighing easily three hundred pounds, sagged outward, held only by the bottom pintle. A blast of heat that made Petra's eyes water instantly leaked from the gap.

"Don't touch it!" Petra shouted as Lenore ran closer to the door. "If that bottom pintle goes, it'll crush you!"

"I can't lose the batch!" Lenore cried, wringing flour-dusted hands. "Petra, fix it! Please!"

Petra looked at the iron. It was grey, dead, and angry.

Lenore was going to lose more than the batch.

Petra had no tools with her. No hammer. No chisel. Nothing.

She looked at Emil. Like always, he had his lute strung along his back

"Can you do it?" she asked. "Can you sing it shut?"

Emil's eyes looked blown.

"I… I can try," he said.

He pulled out the lute. He tried to tune it, but Lenore was chittering about everything that was going wrong that he couldn't hear the strings.

"Quiet!" Petra roared. "Everyone!"

The room went silent, save for the roar of the oven fire.

Emil started to play. He struggled to find the chord, that sturdy, grounding sound that had worked on the nails.

Petra watched the oven door.

Nothing.

The iron didn't hum. It just hung there, heavy and hateful.

"It's not working!" Emil whispered. "I can't hear the resonance. The air… it's too thick?"

"Keep playing!" Petra tried to listen harder. "You're close, I can feel it." Emil's tone, his tune, was almost right.

With a screech, the bottom hinge gave a sickening lurch. The door swung out another inch.

"It's falling!" Lenore gasped.

"Move!" Petra said.

It wasn't Lenore who moved. It was Thom.

The miller, who lived upstairs with Lenore but usually was asleep until noon, launched himself at the oven.

"No!" Petra screamed.

Thom didn't listen. He slammed his mighty shoulder against the burning hot iron door. He grabbed the handle with his gloved hands—leather gardening gloves, not forge mitts—and shoved.

He was a mountain of a man, usually gentle, but now his massive frame was contorted. The oven's handle was too low for him, built for generations of petite bakers. His sandy hair wild; his broad, ruddy face set in a wince as he forced his weight against the iron, knees bent, unlaced boots skidding on the floor.

The reek of burning leather flooded the room. Thom roared in pain, his face turning beet red, but he forced the door back into its frame.

"Can't," he grunted through gritted teeth. "Hold it… forever!"

Smoke was rising from his gloves.

Emil's tune faltered.

Petra looked around wildly. She needed a fix. Not magic. Not music. Physics.

There, by the open fireplace.

"Keep playing!" she yelled to Emil.

She grabbed the rusted pair of tongs from the tool set.

"Lenore, steel!" Petra barked. "Sharpening steel! And something heavy—pestle! Mallet!"

"Counter!"

Petra ran to the counter. She grabbed the honing steel. She grabbed a heavy stone pestle from a mortar, and turned back to the door.

The problem was obvious The knuckles of the hinge were aligned, but the pin was sheared inside.

The heat was blistering. Thom's shoulders shook, sweat pouring down his face.

"Hold on," she said. "Three seconds." She reached into her pocket and her fingers closed around cold, familiar iron. The First Nail.

"Lift!" she ordered. "Align the holes!"

Thom groaned and shifted.

Petra jammed the tip of the honing steel into the hinge, shouting as the heat bit her hand. She struck the handle with the pestle. The broken shard of the old pin popped out the bottom. She let it fall, far too hot to touch.

She barely heard Emil's music, but her body matched his rhythm.

She took the First Nail and lined it up with the door's empty knuckles. She slammed the pestle down. Once. Twice.

The Nail drove home, replacing the pin. It fit perfectly.

Petra dropped the pestle and grabbed the tongs, seizing the protruding point of the nail. It wasn't like the horseshoe, or the hinges, or the nails she'd made. It didn't hum or soften under Emil's song. It was stubborn, dead iron, and it fought her.

With a grunt of effort that strained every tendon in her arm, she bent the metal back on itself, clinching the joint by brute force.

"Let go!" she ordered Thom.

Thom slumped back, cradling his hands.

The door groaned. It sagged against the nail. The iron bent, screeching. But it held.

The door stayed closed.

Silence fell over the bakery. The only sound was Thom's ragged breathing and the pop of the fire in the oven.

Petra stared at the nail. It was ugly. It was bent crooked. It was a scar on the beautiful iron face of the oven.

But it worked.

She backed away from the oven, joining Emil on the other side of the big prep counter.

He was standing, swaying, face lined with pain and panic, the lute hanging limp in his hand.

"I couldn't feel it," he whispered. "It was… empty. Why didn't it work?"

Petra looked at Thom, who was now sitting on the floor while Lenore frantically peeled the burnt gloves off his blistered palms.

She didn't know.

14

The back porch of The Steeping Kettle smelled of late-season rosemary and burnt meat.

Linnea had insisted on moving them outside. "The air is cleaner," she said, her voice tight. "And the light is better."

Now Thom sat on Fen's potter's stool, while Linnea worked on his hands. The big miller's usual ruddy complexion had drained to the color of old parchment. He stared at the horizon, his breath hitching in shallow, wet rasps.

Lenore hovered behind him, vibrating with anxiety, twisting the hem of her flour-dusted apron. "He needs to rest, doesn't he? He can't go back in there."

"Flex," Linnea ordered gently.

Thom tried. His fingers twitched. A fresh bead of sweat rolled down his temple.

Linnea dipped a cloth into a bowl of dark, pungent

liquid. It wasn't magic. Petra knew the smell—aloe, comfrey, and a distilled spirit that made her eyes water from three feet away. Linnea wasn't singing. She wasn't humming. She worked with calm, quiet efficiency.

"The skin is intact on the palms," Linnea said, more to herself than them. "But the heat went deep. Muscles are shocked. Tendons are inflamed."

"I'll just wrap them," Thom wheezed. "When I mill."

"You can't mill," Linnea agreed. She didn't look up. "If you grip a lever today, you'll tear the blisters. If you tear the blisters, you risk infection. If you get an infection in a flour mill..." She trailed off, letting the threat hang.

"You absolutely cannot," Lenore said, her voice shrill. "The flour dust alone..."

Petra stood by the railing. She couldn't see the square from here—the bulk of the tea shop blocked the view—but she could hear it. The low murmur of the Sunday morning crowd drifting over the roof, a dissonance of confused voices. Churchgoers, late risers. They would be staring at the open door of the bakery, wondering where everyone had gone.

They couldn't see the near-disaster. They just saw a interruption to their routine.

Emil sat on the doorsteps. He hadn't spoken since they left the bakery. He held his lute across his lap like a shield, his knuckles white on the neck.

"It works," Petra said. "The door held."

Thom managed a weak grin. "Ugliest repair I've ever seen, smith."

"Temporary," Petra said. "I'll forge a proper pin soon as I can. Cold iron. No fancy tricks."

Emil flinched.

Petra turned back to the bakery. "I need to check the damage."

"Oh!" Lenore said. "And the bread! It must just be coals by now."

Thom's breath hitched as Linnea started wrapping his hands. "Go check. I'll be fine."

Petra crossed the street with Lenore. The cobblestones hard under her boots. Unforgiving.

In the bakery, the scents of scorched leather and burnt bread hung heavy in the air. Lenore blocked the door open to clear the stench, her movements jerky and manic.

"Okay, okay," she muttered. "First batch is gone, but the oven is hot. The second batch is over-proofed. I have to save it. Marda warned me the glass is dropping. Storms make the glass drop. If the pass closes, we need to stock up."

She grabbed a flat wooden paddle and overturned a wicker proofing basket. The dough popped out, soft and spreading too fast. She marched toward the cast iron door.

Then she froze.

Her hand hovered inches from the handle—the same handle that had seared the skin from Thom's palms. She was staring at the ugly, bent First Nail clinched over the hinge.

She didn't reach for the latch. It looked like she couldn't.

"Lenore," Petra said softly.

"I have to put them in," Lenore whispered, her voice trembling. "The yeast won't wait."

But she didn't move. She vibrated, a tuning fork struck too hard.

Petra stepped past her, reached for the handle. Opened the door.

It gave a squeal of protest, but held.

Lenore seemed to wake up. She drove the paddle into the oven, pushing aside the blackened, smoking shapes already there. The smell of char washed over them. She shoved the fresh dough into place, and then scooped the charred loaves out on the paddle.

Petra slammed the door.

Lenore walked with the paddle out the back door, her movements jerky When she came back in, the paddle was bare.

Lenore didn't check the latch. She dropped the paddle and ran back to Thom, across the way.

Petra knelt on the floor, her hands trembling. The broken pieces of the original pin lay in the soot. Two halves of a steel rod, sheared in the middle.

Steel shouldn't snap like this. Not under a static load. It should bend first. It should deform.

She held the shard up to the light of the window.

The break wasn't clean. It wasn't bright, shiny metal.

The center of the rod was black. Pitted. Eaten away.

It looked like a sponge.

Petra felt a chill that had nothing to do with the temperature.

"Rust," she whispered.

This wasn't stress. This wasn't a mechanical failure. The metal had rotted from the inside out.

Why didn't the song work?

If the metal was compromised, the song should have highlighted it. Emil should have heard the dissonance before the snap. That was the whole point of the Singing Forge. To find the flaws. To heal the cracks.

Unless...

Unless they were the flaw.

Had they rushed it? Had the headache behind her eye thrown off the rhythm? Had existing in the same space as Emil—the confused, messy, magnetic tension of him—drowned out the warning?

Or was it something worse?

She pocketed the shards.

She walked back out into the sunlight.

Emil was still on the steps behind the tea shop. He looked up as she approached. His eyes were wide, hollow, blown out by panic.

Petra sat down beside him. The stone was cold against her legs.

"I tried," he whispered.

"I know," she said.

"I played the chord," Emil said. " E suspended. The

one for binding. The one that worked on the nails." He stared at his hands. "I played it perfectly, Petra."

"Maybe the noise…" Petra started. "The panic…"

"No." Emil shook his head. "It wasn't that. I couldn't hear the resonance."

He looked at her, the confusion on his face shadowing into despair.

"No resonance," he said. "I reached out with the music, and there was nothing there. No vibration. No hum. No life."

He swallowed.

"The iron was empty, Petra. It was a void."

Petra touched her pocket, feeling the jagged edge of the corroded pin through the fabric.

"It wasn't empty," she said, grim. "It was dead."

15

The smithy was dark, and cold. Petra lit the oil lamp but not the forge.

She and Emil had helped Linnea get Thom settled in their apartment above the bakery. The big miller had been dosed with Linnea's strongest willow-bark tea and was finally sleeping. Lenore had stopped vibrating, anchored by the weight of keeping him safe. She hadn't even looked up as Petra and Emil slipped out the door.

Emil stood by the anvil. His slim strength looked frail against the mass of the anvil and the deep dark forge. Surrounded by racks of heavy hammers and tongs sized for Petra's hands, not his. His lute was wrapped in its case, leaning against the wall like a prisoner.

Petra pulled the tall stool up to the workbench in front of the front window. She pushed the shutters aside to pull in as much of the pale winter light as possible.

She cleared a space on the high workbench, sweeping aside a schematic for a new gate hinge.

Petra reached into her pocket and pulled out the shards of the pin. She placed them on the wood. They didn't clink. They hissed, a faint, dry sound like sand on glass.

Petra adjusted the oil lamp, pulling the flame higher. She picked up a heavy magnifying glass—usually reserved for checking filigree work—and held it over the metal.

She leaned in.

Under magnification, the damage was hideous.

Normal rust was a surface infection. It flaked. It scaled. It worked from the outside in, catalyzed by moisture and oxygen.

This was different.

The outer skin of the steel rod was intact, shiny and smooth where she had polished it. But the cross-section...

The center was a honeycomb.

The metal looked like bone that had been eaten by marrow rot. Grey, powdery webbing stretched across black voids. The structural integrity was gone. It was a miracle the pin had held as long as it did.

"It ate the heart," Petra said.

"I tried to bind it," Emil's voice was thin, tense. "When I heard the snap, I thought... I thought it was just a stress fracture. Like the ladle we fixed last week."

Petra nodded slowly, looking up at him. “Sonic welding. You vibrate the edges until they fuse.”

“I played the fusion chord,” Emil said. “I pushed the sound right into the break. It should have grabbed. It should have hummed back.”

He picked up a heavy forging hammer from the rack, testing its weight. Petra squelched the urge to shout at him to put it down.

“But the sound didn’t hit anything,” he said. “It didn’t bounce. It just... fell in.”

Petra shrugged, hands up in surrender. “There was nothing to weld,” she said. “You can’t fuse dust, Emil.”

She picked up one of the shards. So light. So wrong.

“The Rust isn’t just eating the metal,” she said. “It’s eating the part of the metal that listens to you. To us. It’s eating the resonance.”

Emil dropped the hammer. It hit the dirt floor with a dull thud.

“Then I’m useless to you,” he said. “If I can’t sing to it... if the iron won’t listen...” He looked at his hands, untouched by the fire. “Then I’m just noise, Petra. And you can’t build a gate, a latch, a tool out of noise.”

“No,” Petra said.

She didn’t move to the forge. She didn’t reach for a tool. She just stood there, gripping the edge of the workbench until her knuckles turned white.

“You aren’t noise, Emil,” she whispered. She looked down at the honeycomb rot in her hand. “But I think... I think I am.”

Emil frowned. "You?"

She spun on the stool to face him. "Look at it," she said, thrusting the shard toward him. "It's hollow. The core is gone because the magic couldn't find anything to hold onto." She tappped her own chest, the sound dull and flat in the quiet room. "Just like me."

The admission hung in the air, heavier than the anvil. For months, she had been pretending the exhaustion was just physical. Just the cost of keeping the valley running. But looking at the honeycomb rot, she recognized the pattern. She felt it in herself. A weakness, a brittleness. One good hit, and she would simply crumble.

"That's not true," Emil said, stepping closer.

In the light of the oil lamp, he looked thin, ghostlike. New lines—exhaustion—circled his eyes, and there were faint cracks in his usual calm. His students were running him ragged in the mornings, and then Petra's need was draining him in the afternoons. But his gaze was steady.

"You're the strongest person I know," he said.

"I'm not," she said, her voice cracking. "Sometime—I don't know when, it was gradual, maybe. I stopped forging. No, I stopped putting myself into the metal. When the trouble came, I let your song do the heavy lifting. I let the magic fill the gaps where my soul used to be." She felt the tears prickling, hot and sudden. "And now the magic is gone, and there's nothing left but a shell."

Emil reached out, his hand hovering over hers. He didn't touch her, just stood ready.

"Then we fill it," he said softly.

Petra looked up.

"We fill the shell," Emil said. "If the magic won't hold, we use something else."

Petra took his hand. His skin so soft, and warm. And strong. She squeezed it. He squeezed back. A spark of something, hot and bright, flared in her chest. It wasn't magic. It was just... connection. And it was enough.

Petra looked at the dead forge. She looked at the rack of cold steel.

"Iron," she whispered.

"Iron," Emil agreed. "And sweat. And muscle." He lifted both their hands, and reached for her face. With both their hands, he wiped a tear away from her cheek.

For a moment, Petra sighed into the touch. Then she let go, and stood. She walked to the coal scuttle. She grabbed the shovel. The rattle of the stones was loud, aggressive. A promise.

"We do it the old way," she said, throwing the coal into the firepot. "No songs. No currents."

"Why?" Emil asked. "If the magic is gone, why not call it back?"

"Because the Song opens the metal," Petra said. She looked at the honeycomb rot. "It makes the iron soft. Compliant. It creates space for the magic to flow. But when the magic fails... the Rust fills the gap."

She struck a match. The flame flared, blindingly bright.

"The Rust didn't eat the magic, Emil. It ate the empty space."

She tossed the match into the kindling. The smoke curled up, grey and biting.

"So we stop making space," she said. "We use force. We use weight. We hammer the iron so tight, so dense, that there is no room for the rot to enter. Cold Iron."

"Cold Iron," Emil whispered. He looked at the silent anvil, then at his own fine hands. The words felt heavy on his tongue. Dead.

Petra ignored the warning in her heart and pointed to the bellows handle. "Help pump?"

The hammer came down with a dull, bone-jarring thud.

Petra gritted her teeth against the shockwave that traveled up the handle, through her wrist, and slammed into her shoulder.

Wrong. Wrong. *Wrong*.

For six days, the forge had sung. A strike was a question, and the anvil's ring was the answer—a bright, resonant hum that vibrated in Petra's teeth and settled in her bones. For six days, the metal had moved like clay, eager to be shaped.

Now, it was just dead weight.

Again.

Petra gritted her teeth. She twisted the tongs, flipping the heavy bar of stock. Somehow,it felt even more dense and sullen, fighting her every inch of the way. She raised the hammer again. Her shoulder screamed, a hot, tearing line of pain that she hadn't felt since before Emil. Since before the music.

Wham.

"Heat!" she barked.

To her left, Emil scrambled. He grabbed the handle of the great bellows and pulled.

The air sputtered. The coals glowed a dull, angry red, but they didn't roar. Emil pulled again, his entire body weight hanging off the lever. He looked a wreck. His white shirt was stained grey with soot and sweat. His hair was plastered to his forehead. His hands—those long, clever musician's fingers—were wrapped in strips of torn rag, trying to protect them from the heat and the friction.

He wasn't built for this. He was built for precision, for the delicate tension of a lute string. Not the brute agony of pumping air into a dying fire.

"Harder," Petra snapped, hating herself. "I'm losing the color."

She normally worked the bellows herself—pump, heat, strike, repeat. A solitary rhythm. But this iron was different. It was dead. Without the song to keep the resonance alive, the heat bled out the moment the metal left the coals. If she stopped hammering to pump, she lost the temper. She needed him. Even if he was bad at it.

Emil nodded, not wasting breath on words. He hauled on the lever. Wheeze. Roar.

Better.

Petra thrust the metal back into the heart of the fire. She leaned against the anvil, gasping for air. The heat in the small room was suffocating. The air shared space with sulfur and old sweat.

The door creaked open. Not Emil's weight—lighter. Hesitant.

"Petra?" Linnea's voice, soft as always. She held a covered mug, steam curling from beneath the lid. "I brought you something. Chamomile and honey. For the—"

"Not now." Petra didn't look up. "I'm working."

"You've been working for six hours. You should—"

"I said not now."

A pause. Then the door clicked shut.

Petra's hands tightened on the tongs. She didn't have time for tea. She didn't deserve tea. Not until the iron was fixed. Not until she'd proven she could still do this without magic, without music, without anyone.

She pulled the piece back and banged it onto the anvil. The hinge pin for the bakery oven. The replacement for the one that had snapped.

It was ugly.

The metal was thick, beaten into shape with violence rather than persuasion. The surface was pitted where she had hammered too hard. The lines were uneven. It looked like something an apprentice would make in their first week, not the work of the Valley's best smith.

But it was solid.

Noticing her silence, Emil paused. "Is it… is it ready?" he asked. His voice rasped. He leaned against the bellows frame, his chest heaving.

Petra put the pin back in the fire. Make it white-hot.

"One more pass," she said. "To harden the skin."

She moved to the swage block, to check the fit. She didn't hum. She didn't tap a rhythm. she just hit it.

Wham. Wham. Wham.

Each blow was a punishment. For being weak. For relying on magic. For letting herself get soft.

The metal cooled to a dull cherry, then to grey. Petra dropped it into the oil quench. It hissed—a violent screech, not the musical sigh of the water quench—and a cloud of black smoke billowed up.

She coughed, waving the smoke away. She fished the pin out with the tongs and held it up.

It was a lump. A heavy, black lump of iron.

"Done," she said.

Emil pushed himself off the wall. He stumbled a little, catching himself on the workbench. He came to look.

"It looks... strong," he offered.

"It looks like a brick," Petra said. She tossed it onto the bench. It hit with a heavy thunk that made the tools rattle . "But it won't rot. It's too dense. There's no room for anything to get in."

She stripped off her heavy leather gloves. Her hands shook. Not the fine tremor of adrenaline, but the coarse shake of muscle failure. She hid them behind her back, pretending she needed them to help arch her back as she stretched.

"We need to do the gate latch next," she said. "And the mill wheel reinforcement."

Emil looked at the window. The light was fading. "Petra. It's been six hours. You've done four commissions. You can barely stand."

"No time. Storm's coming."

As if on cue, the shutters rattled.

It wasn't a normal wind. Even inside, insulated by two feet of stone, Petra could feel the pressure drop. The wind whined around the chimney cap, a high, thin sound like a dog begging to be let in.

"We have time," Emil said. He reached for the water jug. His hand shook so badly he spilled half of it before he could get the cup to his lips.

Petra watched him. He looked grey. The soot accentuated the hollows of his cheeks. A ghost haunting a coal mine.

Guilt, sharp and cold, pierced through her exhaustion.

"Go home, Emil," she said.

He froze, cup halfway from his mouth. "What?"

"You're done," she said. She turned away, picking up a rag to wipe down the anvil. "You're slowing me down. I can pump the bellows myself."

"I'm helping," he said, putting the cup down with a clack. "You can't work the iron and the fire at the same time. Not with cold iron. That's what you said"

"I did it for twenty years before you showed up," Petra said, looking down so he couldn't see the lie. She scrubbed at a spot of soot on the anvil face, scrubbing until the metal shone. "I don't need a bellows-boy. I need a smith. And you aren't one."

The silence that followed was louder than the hammer.

"Is that what I am?" Emil asked, oddly quiet. "A bellows-boy?"

Petra didn't turn around. If she looked at him—at his rag-wrapped hands, at the exhaustion she had put there —she would break. And she couldn't break.

She had to be iron.

"The magic is gone," she said to the anvil. "And you aren't strong enough to be a striker. So what else is there?"

She heard him take a breath. A shaky, ragged sound.

"I see," he said.

He didn't argue. He didn't fight back. He just walked to the corner and picked up his lute case. He swung it onto his back—carefully, so carefully—and walked to the door.

He reached for the handle.

The wind grabbed the door and slammed it against the wall with a crack like a rifle shot. A roar of sound—white noise and fury—drowned out the world. A bitter metallic scent rushed in, ice and fury.

For a heartbeat, the fire banked down, the red coals dimming as the gale sucked the oxygen from the room. Then they flared back up, angry and wild.

Leaves and grit swirled into the room.

"Petra!"

It wasn't Emil.

Ferdie stood in the doorway, fighting to hold the heavy oak panel against the gale. The courier looked windblown and wild, his cap gone, his coat flapping.

"Ferdie?" Petra turned.

"Close up!" Ferdie shouted over the wind. "Council's orders!"

"I'll stay here," Petra said.

"No!" Ferdie yelled. "It's a whiteout. Coming down the valley. The barometer at the station broke the glass! Marda says everyone to the Hall. Now!"

He looked at Emil, who stood frozen by the door.

"Grab your kit. We're locking down the school and the shops. Everyone sleeps in the Hall tonight."

Emil looked back, at Petra. Held out a hand.

Petra looked away, at the pile of cold iron on the bench. The ugly pin. The un-fixed latches.

"Go," she said to Emil. "Help Ferdie. I have to bank the fire."

"Petra—"

"Go!" she barked. She grabbed her heavy tongs and turned her back on him. "I'll be right behind you."

Emil hesitated. She felt him looking at her. Heard him turn and go

Ferdie was still there. "You're coming, right?"

"Ten minutes," she said

Ferdie nodded and vanished into the grey swirl. When the door slammed shut, it was as if the storm had vanished.

But only for a moment.

The wind howled. The shutters banged again, and again.

She was alone.

Petra walked to the fire. She should bank it. She should cover the coals and leave.

Instead, she picked up the hammer.

She looked at the unfinished bar for the mill wheel.

"One more," she whispered to the empty room. "Just one more."

She thrust the metal into the dying coals and started to pump the bellows.

Wheeze. Cough.

It was hard. It was so hard.

But it was better than the silence.

16

Twenty minutes later, Petra stepped out of the smithy and into a wall of white.

It wasn't snow. Snow fell. Snow drifted. This was a physical assault. The wind didn't howl; it screamed, a high, tearing sound that vibrated in her teeth. It drove the ice crystals horizontally, scouring the stone outer walls of the smithy and stripping the breath from her lungs.

She gasped, choking on the cold. Ancient ice, a flavor so sharp it felt like biting into a coin. She turned to check the latch on the forge door. Solid, already stiff from the cold.

A gust of wind slammed her into the door.

She had to move.

She pushed away from the wall, keeping her center of gravity low. The yard was a white wilderness, the familiar path to the street erased. She waded through already drifting snow, her breath coming in ragged gasps that froze instantly in the air. It was only twenty feet to the edge of the property, but in this wind, it felt like miles.

She had to get to the Village Hall. The wind was bad here, but inside, the thick stone walls would hold. The hearth would keep the chill at bay. It was the only safe place left.

She made it past the inn by hugging the porch, her shoulder pressed against the rough-hewn timber. The wood was cold, but it was solid. It didn't move. It didn't groan.

But there were two more blocks to cover. And she had to cross the street. The open square was a wind tunnel, and the Hall was on the other side.

Something slapped against the railing, against her hip. A heavy, tarred rope, knotted around the porch support.

The walk-lines. Ferdie. He must have run them before the weather broke.

Petra grabbed the line. Already stiff with ice, hard as cable. She kept one hand on the rough fibers, using it to haul herself hand over hand forward against the wind. Step by windy, icy step. Past the grocer, past the space where the market stalls usually stood, past the village well. Past the seamstresses shops, past the tea shop. On and on and on.

After what felt like half a day, the rope ended at what must be the side gate to the Hall, the one that led to the alley.

Except there was no gate there.

She had repaired its hinge earlier. A thick slab of cold iron, ugly but functional.

It was gone.

No, not gone.

Petra knelt in the drift, shielding her eyes against the stinging grit. The wind lifted a moment, and she could see. The hinge hadn't bent. It hadn't twisted under the wind's torque.

It had shattered.

Jagged shards of grey metal lay in the snow, looking like broken pottery. The break lines were crystalline, bright and sharp.

"Brittle," she whispered into her scarf.

The word was swallowed by the wind, but the knowledge settled in her gut like a stone. Cold iron was hard. It was dense. But it had no give. Without the Song to align the grain, without the resonance to let the metal breathe and flex, it couldn't handle the shock. It was just dead weight against a live force.

And the Village Hall…

The Hall was held together by iron. Iron that had been forged centuries ago by the First Smith.

Not by her.

Lucky for everyone.

Petra scrambled to her feet. The wind caught her, shoving her sideways. She didn't walk; she leaned into the gale, fighting for every step.

~

The Village Hall was a whale of a building, a massive structure of timber and stone that had anchored the north side of the square for three hundred years. Its slate roof was steep, designed to shed the heavy mountain snows, and its walls were three feet of fieldstone.

Usually, it smelled of floor wax and old paper, with a dusting of casseroles past. Tonight, as Petra shouldered through the heavy double doors and then helped two of Marda's stable hands force them shut against the gale, the predominant scents were wet wool, damp dog, and hot cider.

Finally, the latch dropped with a heavy thud that vibrated through the floorboards. Inside, the roar of the wind dropped to a dull, omnipresent rumble. It sounded like they were inside a drum that was being beaten by a giant.

The main hall was full of motion. Lanterns hung from the rafters, casting a warm, golden light that successfully held back the violence outside.

Families clustered on blankets, staking out small territories of comfort. The chandler's family had pushed two benches together to make a crib for the baby. Elder Gretch was sitting on a crate, clutching his prize hen, explaining to a fascinated toddler why feathers were better than fur.

Marda stood in the center of the back of the room,

near the great hearth. The innkeeper wasn't a general tonight; she was the hostess of the valley's most crowded dinner party.

"You, blankets to the widow Gretch," she called out, her voice cheerful. "And get that fire built up—we have enough wood to roast an ox! Is the soup ready?"

"Almost!" Lenore called from a small side area that had been cleared for a kitchen. The baker, flushed and fluttering, sliced loaves of bread with efficient, practiced strokes. "And the rolls are warm!" Her flour-dusted apron made a stark contrast to the dark wool of the crowd.

Petra peeled off her scarf. Her face felt raw, wind-burned and stinging, but the air in here was soft.

She stood by the door, dripping onto the floorboards, feeling like an intruder. People were finding comfort in closeness, in the shared warmth of the herd. They had weathered storms before. They knew the drill: Hunker down, eat soup, wait it out.

But Petra felt cold. Cold deep in her marrow.

She saw the shattered hinge in her mind.

Was the village rejecting her? Recalling the magic of the First Smith?

She shivered. She scanned the room for Emil.

He'd washed the coal dust off and now sat on a crate near the hearth with some of the younger children. He had his lute out. He was playing a low, rolling folk tune—"The River Runs South"—that had the kids chirping along as their elder siblings and parents tried to get everything settled.

It was a small sound, barely audible over the rumble of the wind, but it was steady. Maybe it was as big as he could make it, right now. Emil looked exhausted, his face grey, his eyes shadowed. But his hands—mauled and bandaged—moved with gentle precision.

He was helping. He was weaving a blanket of sound to match Marda's wool ones.

Petra didn't go to him. She couldn't. Not while the math in her head was screaming.

She walked the perimeter of the room. She needed to see the bones of the beast.

The walls were solid fieldstone. They wouldn't fail. But the roof…

She looked up.

The roof was a masterpiece of timber framing—massive oak trusses rising into the shadows. But oak shifted. Oak breathed. To keep the heavy timbers connected, the First Smith had forged iron straps to wrap the joints. And to keep the fieldstone walls from bowing out under the crushing weight of the snow and the suction of the wind, he had installed iron tie-rods. Thick black bars that ran along the walls, pinning the structure together.

They looked solid. To anyone else, they looked like permanent features of the world, as immutable as the mountains.

But Petra knew iron. And she knew silence.

She placed her gloved hand against the stone wall where the North Rod anchored. The stone was cold.

She stripped off the glove. She pressed her bare palm against the metal bracket.

It was vibrating.

A high, thin tremor ran through the iron.

Not a hum. Not the warm resonance of the Singing Forge. A scream. A frequency of tension so high it set her teeth on edge.

"Loud, isn't it?"

Petra jumped, pulling her hand back.

Fen stood next to her. The potter was wrapped in a grey wool blanket, their arms crossed. They weren't looking at the people. They weren't looking at the soup or the fire. They were looking at the wall.

"You can feel it?" Petra asked.

"I can hear it," Fen said. Their voice was quiet, direct. "The clay in the walls is complaining. It doesn't like being pulled."

Petra looked back at the bracket. "The rods are taking too much load. The wind isn't just pushing; it's lifting. It's trying to suck the roof off like a lid. The iron is the only thing holding it down."

Fen nodded. They reached out and touched the stone, their fingers seeking the grain of the mortar. "The mortar is strong. It's not crumbling. The walls are holding their ground."

The stone wouldn't give. So the iron had to take it all.

"The iron is old," Petra said.

"Will it hold?" Fen asked.

Petra looked at the black bar stretching across the lantern-lit space. Thirty feet of iron. It had held for three centuries. Through blizzards. Through spring thaws.

But the First Smith had sung this iron. He had poured his Intent into it.

And now the valley was silent. The Rust had eaten the resonance.

Petra pictured the shattered gate. The way the metal had simply given up.

"It… should?" she said.

Fen looked at her. Their dark eyes were unreadable, but they didn't look convinced.

Above them, the wind gusted. A massive, invisible hand slapped the side of the building.

The Hall groaned. A deep creak that came from the bones of the structure. The lanterns swayed. The vibration under Petra's hand spiked, sharp and jagged.

Fen flinched.

"The clay is stubborn," Fen whispered. "It won't let go."

Petra looked at the crowd. At Marda's daughter serving soup. At Emil playing his heartbeat song. At the infants sleeping in a pile of blankets.

They thought they were safe. They trusted that the stone and the iron would protect them.

Petra put her glove back on, hiding her trembling hand.

"We need to watch the North rod," she said. "If it goes…"

"If it goes, the roof spreads," Fen finished. "And the walls come down."

"Yes."

They stood together in the shadows, two artisans listening to the building scream, while the rest of the village ate bread and soup, unaware that danger could be inside as well as out.

~

Something was wrong in the kitchen.

It wasn't a sound. The Hall was full of sounds—the chatter of families, the clink of spoons, the steady plink of Emil's lute. It was a smell.

Or the lack of one.

Petra left Fen by the wall and moved toward the makeshift kitchen area near the hearth. Marda's younger daughter was still ladling soup, her face flushed with the heat of the fire and the effort of projected cheer. Next to her, Linnea stood over a small copper brazier, staring at a pot of water.

It was boiling. Aggressive white plumes of steam rose into the rafters, vanishing into the gloom. The water roiled, a rolling boil that should have filled the corner with humidity.

But Linnea made no move to pour it.

"Is the water bad?" Petra asked, keeping her voice low so Marda wouldn't hear.

Linnea looked up. Her eyes, usually the warmth of weak tea, were dark. Her hands were clenched in the pockets of her apron. "The water is fine. Plenty hot."

On the table next to the brazier, a small pile of dried leaves waited. Lemon balm. Valerian. Chamomile. The 'Calm Down' blend that Linnea prescribed for everything from colicky babies to nervous grooms. Petra could smell the herbs—dusty, earthy, pungent.

Linnea picked up a pinch of the leaves. Her fingers trembled. She dropped them into the boiling water.

Usually, the leaves would catch the current. They would swirl, hydrate, and sink, releasing their oils into the water. The liquid would turn amber within seconds.

Today, they just floated.

"It's not taking," Linnea whispered. She poked the leaves with a wooden spoon. They bobbed away, refusing to submerge.

"Maybe it's too hot?" Petra asked.

"No," Linnea said. She looked at Petra, and the fear in her face was worse than the wind outside. "There's no Intent. The water... it's scared, Petra. The whole valley is holding its breath."

Petra looked at the floating leaves. The water was rejecting them. It had closed itself off.

What had Fen said? *The clay is stubborn. It won't let go.*

"The valley is out of balance," Linnea said, her voice shaking. "Again." She looked at the stiff leaves. "When I first came here, my protection charm drained the magic like a leak in a bucket. It left everything flat and grey. But this isn't a leak, Petra. It's a flood."

Petra felt a chill that had nothing to do with the draft from the door. She glared up at the black iron tie-rods holding up the roof. Solid metal, forged centuries ago.

She had thought the iron was failing because the magic had drained out of it, leaving it hollow. Like the bakery pin. Like the rust.

But Linnea was suggesting something worse.

The iron wasn't hollow. It was dissolving.

The Song of the First Smith had created resonance. Space within the metal for strength and flexibility to coexist. Intent was the breath in the lungs of the iron.

But all this fear...

The weight of the storm. The screaming wind. The terror of three hundred people huddled in the dark.

It had slammed those spaces shut. The iron had gone rigid. It was holding its breath, just like the water. And rigid things, under pressure, don't bend.

A question rose in her mind, sharp and cold as the draft.

Whose breath?

The First Smith was dust. The Old Songs were just echoes. The iron didn't need a memory.

It needed a voice. A living, present intent.

Whose?

Petra looked at her hands. Callused. Strong. Silent.

When had she stopped putting herself into the metal?

When had she started just hammering instead of humming?

The bakery pin. The gate latch. Every piece she had made since… since the summer, when the work got to be too much. When she'd pushed too hard, burned too bright, and felt the resonance shatter inside her own chest.

She had been forging scared ever since. Closed. Holding her breath.

Just like the iron.

The realization settled over her like wet snow. Cold. Heavy. Suffocating.

The iron couldn't wait for the magic to come back.

Maybe the valley needed a new smith. A new voice. Someone whose song hadn't already shattered.

17

The wind didn't let up. It settled into a rhythm, a deep, thrumming bass note that vibrated in the floorboards and rattled the heavy iron hinges of the doors.

Inside, the village hall was a pocket of defiance. Marda had turned the event into a mini festival . There was soup—thick, potato-leek broth that smelled of earth and comfort—and Lenore's rolls were still warm. Emil was playing an old reel now, something fast and repetitive that kept the children clapping.

But Petra couldn't clap. She couldn't eat.

She stood near the wall, her back against the cold stone, Linnea's words still ringing in her ears. The valley was out of balance. But this time, there was no charm to smash. No simple fix.

Just a smith whose song had already shattered.

In the corner, babies slept in their shared makeshift

crib. Older men played cards at a table, their voices low. Children chased each other around the room, their laughter echoing off the walls.

Above them all, the iron holding the roof together was groaning. Dissolving. The fear had flooded its joins, its edges, and the resonance that once held it together was draining away.

The valley needed a smith who could sing to the iron, who could mend what was broken.

Time to move on. Make way. Give over to a stronger smith, one who would share the village's intent and not freeze up.

The thought should have hurt. Instead, it just felt true.

"Petra?"

Emil's voice was soft. He had put down his lute and crossed the room to her corner, stepping carefully over sleeping children. His face was pale, the shadows under his eyes deep enough to hold water. But his smile was warm

He held out a bowl. "Soup. Lenore said you haven't eaten."

The steam rose between them, carrying the scent of home. Of hope. Of everything she was about to lose. Of everything she already had

"Thanks, but not hungry."

"Petra." He stepped closer. Close enough that she could feel the warmth radiating off him, could catch the faint whiff of pine needles and woodsmoke from the hearth. "You've been standing here for an hour. Just staring at the ceiling."

"I'm watching the roof."

"That's not an answer."

He was looking at her with that expression. The one that made her chest ache. Like she was something worth paying attention to. Like she mattered. After all day today—the failed forging, the shattered metal, the silence that had stretched between them when the magic refused to come—he should have given up on her.

But here he was. Offering soup.

It was worse than anger. Worse than disappointment. His hope was a knife, and she didn't have the heart to tell him she was already bleeding.

"Emil." Her voice came out rough. "You should go back. The children need you."

"The children are fine." He set the bowl on a nearby crate, freeing his hands. "What about you?"

His bandaged fingers brushed her arm. The touch was light—barely there—but it burned.

She flinched.

Emil's face flickered. Hurt. Confusion. He pulled back, and Petra wanted to scream. Wanted to grab his hand and hold it against her cheek and tell him everything—about the Rust, about the iron, about the hollow place inside her chest where the forge-song used to live.

But what could she say? She was broken. The valley needed someone who wasn't.

"I'm sorry," she whispered. "I just—"

"It's fine." His voice was careful now. Flat. "I'll leave the soup. In case you change your mind."

He turned away from her

And that was when the ping came.

The sound was small. A sharp, high note, like a fingernail flicking a crystal glass.

It cut through the rumble of the wind, the chatter of the crowd, and the sudden silence between them.

Petra stopped breathing.

Emil froze mid-step.

Fen, halfway across the room checking a window shutter, went perfectly still.

"What was that?" Marda asked, looking up from a ladle of soup.

The building moaned. Not the creak of timber settling, but a wail of wood fibers tearing under impossible load.

High above, in the shadows of the central truss, a shadow detached itself.

It fell.

It struck the floorboards in the center of the aisle with a thud that shook the benches.

It rolled, heavy and uneven, coming to rest at the feet of Elder Gretch.

A bolt. The size of a man's fist. The threaded end was bright and sheared clean.

The Hall went silent.

Everyone looked up.

The main crossbeam—the massive oak trunk that

spanned the width of the hall—was still in place. But Petra's eyes went straight to the north wall, to the ironwork that held the beam's end secure. She knew it well. She'd inspected it herself two winters back.

An iron bracket, forged by the First Smith, bolted into the stone—a plate as wide as her palm with two holes for the mounting bolts. An iron strap, thick as two fingers, wrapped over the beam and pinned to the bracket with bolts the size of her thumb. Together, they kept the beam seated against the wall. Without them, the crossbeam would slide outward under the weight of the roof, pushing the walls apart. Fifty tons of slate and timber would drop straight down.

The strap hung loose now. One bolt was gone—that was the piece on the floor. The other bolt was still in place, but the bracket was pulling away from the stone, torquing under the full weight of the beam.

Even from here she could see it. The iron was bowing. Bright lines of stress fractures ran across the strap like veins.

It wouldn't hold.

Without the bracket to keep the beam seated, the building groaned. Louder. A grinding sound of stone sliding against stone.

"The roof!" someone screamed.

"It's coming down!"

Panic, sharp and instant, shattered the warmth. A woman grabbed her baby and scrambled backward, knocking over a bench. People surged toward the doors —toward the whiteout that would kill them in minutes.

"No!" Ferdie shouted, throwing his weight against the main doors. "You can't go out there!"

"We'll be crushed!"

"The walls are moving!"

Petra didn't scream. She didn't run.

Thirty feet up, the strap was sliding off the beam, sliver by sliver. As it slipped, the crossbeam would push outward, and the walls would follow.

If the walls moved an inch, the roof would lose its seat.

"People!" Marda barked. "To the walls! Under the balcony! Clear the floor!"

Emil was already moving, herding children and adults alike toward the edges of the room.

Fen loped up to her. The potter had their tools slung over their shoulder.

"Needs a pin," Fen said.

"It needs a clamp," Petra corrected. "It needs to be pulled back together."

"Can't pull that," Fen said. "Five tons of tension, at least."

"We have to try."

Fen looked up, and then back at Petra. She suddenly remembered that Fen was afraid of heights.

Down to one, then. She held her hand out for their tools.

They handed her the tool belt.

Petra slung it over her shoulder—the weight of it familiar, grounding—and ran. Not for the door. For the back corner, where a wooden ladder led up to the maintenance catwalk. From there, she could follow the catwalk along the crossbeams to the north wall, to the failing bracket.

"Petra!" Emil's voice cut through the chaos. She glanced back. He was herding a group of children toward the wall, but his eyes were on her. "Where are you going?"

"Up!" she yelled. "Keep them clear!"

His face went white. For a heartbeat, she thought he would argue. Would try to stop her.

Instead, he nodded. Once. Sharp.

Then she was at the ladder, and there was no more time for goodbyes.

The first rung was slick with condensation. Her boot slipped. She caught herself, fingers biting into the splintered wood, and hauled herself up. Hand over hand. Rung after rung. Her shoulders burned. Her forearms screamed. The tool belt swung against her hip, threatening to throw off her balance.

Don't look down.

She looked down.

Twenty feet of empty air. Thirty. The crowd below was a sea of moving, upturned faces—pale ovals in the lamplight, mouths open in silent screams she couldn't hear over the roar of blood in her ears.

She focused on the patterns they formed, tried to stop

thinking of how small and fragile they were. Emil had gotten most of them against the walls. Good. The center of the floor was clear.

Clear for falling debris.

Clear for her, if she slipped.

She kept climbing.

The air changed as she rose. The cold draft from the doors gave way to trapped heat—body warmth and lamp smoke and the acrid tang of stressed timber. It tasted like a forge fire gone wrong. Like metal pushed too far.

The building groaned again. The ladder shuddered in her grip.

It wasn't going to hold. She wasn't going to make it. She was broken, remember? The valley needed someone whose song hadn't already shattered.

She gritted her teeth and climbed faster.

The catwalk was a narrow wooden plank, maybe eight inches wide, that ran the length of the building at rafter height. It swayed when she pulled herself onto it. The wood creaked. Dust sifted down through the cracks.

She steadied herself, one hand on the rough beam above her head. Her heart was hammering so hard she could feel it in her throat.

The swaying iron bar was ten feet away.

She could see the damage now. The loose end of the tie-rod dangled, the sheared bolt hole empty and ragged. The other end—the one still attached—was bowing under the impossible load. The remaining bolt was a dark nub of metal, threads stripped, barely seated in the bracket.

Even as she watched, she saw it shift. A quarter inch. Maybe less.

The walls groaned in response. A grinding shriek of stone against stone.

The gap between the broken ends was getting wider.

Two minutes. Maybe less.

One bolt. Five tons of tension. And her.

Petra stepped onto the swaying plank. She had no rope. She had no harness. She had Fen's tools and her own two hands and the knowledge that if she failed, the sky would fall on everyone she loved.

18

The catwalk shivered beneath her feet.

The plank was eight inches wide. Felt like less. Old oak, gray with age, dry enough to dissolve but so thick it never would. It ran along the crossbeams toward the north wall, ending at the failing bracket. On either side: nothing. A thirty-foot drop to the stone floor. The only handholds were the crossbeams themselves—massive oak trunks, rough-hewn, spaced every six feet. She could reach them if she stretched. If she didn't slip.

Ten feet ahead, where the catwalk met the north wall, the iron bracket clung to the stone. Above it, the iron strap that should have been wrapped tight over the crossbeam hung loose, one bolt gone, the other barely holding. The massive oak beam it was meant to secure creaked with every gust that battered the shutters below.

The wind screamed past the slate tiles, pushed against the walls where they attached to the roof, trying to get purchase and pry the building apart. Inside, the trapped heat from the bodies below rose in waves, but way up here in the rafters, the air was cold. Sharp. Dusty, and tainted with the acrid smell of wood fibers tearing under strain.

She crouched low, knees against the plank, and opened Fen's tool belt.

Awl. Pliers. A wooden wedge, the kind potters used to brace kiln shelves. A small hammer. A coil of wire.

The building moaned. A deep, bone-shaking sound that vibrated down the catwalk and into her chest. The plank swayed—just a fraction—and she grabbed the beam beside her, fingers scraping across the rough bark. Splinters bit into the pads of her fingers. Small price, when the alternative was falling.

Below, someone screamed. A child crying. Marda's voice, sharp and yet calm, cutting through the noise.

Petra pressed her forehead against the cold wood. Breathed. The beam was solid. Ancient. It had held this roof for a hundred years. More.

It would hold her.

Move.

She crawled forward on hands and knees, keeping her weight centered, one palm flat against the plank and the other reaching ahead for the next crossbeam. The gap between beams felt infinite—six feet of nothing but air and the distant flicker of lamplight far below. Frost had crept through the cracks, leaving white feathers of ice on the timber. Cold seeped through her shirt, her trousers, her skin.

Every creak of the structure echoed in her chest like a skipped heartbeat. Every gust of wind made the catwalk shiver.

The bracket was close now. She could see the rust blooming across the iron like a bruise. Smell that dead, metallic dust that had been eating the valley's metal for months.

The ironwork was worse than she'd feared. The strap that should have been solid was pitted and gray, the forge-scale flaking away in patches. The iron beneath looked wrong. Porous. Like bone left too long in vinegar.

The sheared bolt had torn a ragged hole in the bracket where it met the stone, the edges bright and sharp where they'd given way. The strap hung loose, no longer pinning the beam to the wall. The remaining bolt was a dark nub of metal, barely seated in the bracket, threads almost visibly stripping with every creak of the roof.

She had seconds. Maybe less.

The wedge first. If she could brace the strap back against the beam, take some of the tension off the remaining bolt—

She jammed the wedge into the gap between iron and timber. Pushed. The wood bit into the metal, holding for a moment—

The iron crumbled.

Not cracked. Not bent. Crumbled. Like ash. The Rust had eaten it hollow from the inside.

The wedge slipped. Fell. She heard it clang against the floor far below—distant, muffled by the roar of blood in her ears.

No screams. Good. People were against the walls. Clear.

She grabbed the awl. Tried to jam it into the open bolt hole as a temporary pin, something to keep the bracket from sliding off entirely.

The iron fell apart around it. Dust sifted through her fingers, gray and dead.

Too brittle. The Rust had taken everything.

"Emil!" She screamed it. Her throat tore with the force of it. "The binding tune! Play it!"

Below, she could see him. A pale face in the lamplight, turned up toward her. His lute was in his hands. He nodded. She saw his fingers move across the strings.

She couldn't hear a note.

The wind. The groaning of the building. The roar in her own ears—blood pounding, breath rasping, the desperate hammer of her heart. It swallowed everything.

She screamed again. "Emil! I need you!"

His mouth moved. He was shouting something back. She couldn't hear.

He was too far away.

The building shuddered. A deep, grinding vibration that ran up through the catwalk and into her bones. The walls were shifting. She could feel it—the slow, inexorable spread of the roof beams pushing outward, searching for a gap, a weakness, a way to fall.

The remaining bolt gave.

It didn't shear clean like the first. It twisted. Shrieked. The threads screamed against the bracket, metal against metal, and then it popped free and tumbled into the dark.

The strap started to drop.

Petra lunged.

Her hands closed around the iron strap—cold, dead, dusty under her palms but with some integrity yet. She pulled. Hauled the loose end back over the beam. Her shoulders screamed. Her arms shook. The weight of the crossbeam was pushing outward, and she was the only thing holding the strap in place.

She braced her feet against the catwalk. Leaned back. Held.

The strap stopped sliding.

The building stopped groaning.

For one impossible moment, everything was still.

Then the weight hit her.

It wasn't gradual. It was sudden, total, crushing. The full weight of the crossbeam pressing outward, transferred through the strap into her arms, her shoulders, her back. Every muscle fiber stretched to breaking. Her vision grayed at the edges. Her lungs forgot how to breathe.

She held.

She was the only thing between the roof and her people. The only thing keeping fifty tons of slate and timber from dropping into the room where Emil stood, where Marda was sheltering children, where Fen and Ferdie and Lenore and Thom and everyone waited for her to save them from the sky falling in.

The Anchor.

The thought came unbidden. Her mother's voice, or maybe her father's. *You've always been the anchor, Petra. The one who holds when everyone else lets go.*

Anchors don't sing. Anchors don't dance. Anchors just—

Hold.

Her arms shook. Her fingers were going numb. The cold of the iron was seeping into her bones, spreading up through her wrists, her elbows, her shoulders. She could smell the Rust. Taste it.

She could feel it now. The Dissonance. The fear that had flooded the valley, that had eaten the iron from the inside out. It was in her too, she realized. It had been in her for months. Since her too-busy summer, since her forge went cold, since she stopped believing she had anything left to give.

She was the broken pin. The iron was dead because she was dead, inside. Hollow. Empty.

Below, Emil was still playing. She could see his hands moving, his mouth shaped around words she couldn't hear. He was trying. They were all trying.

But she was alone up here. Alone with the dead iron and the screaming wind and the crushing weight of everything she couldn't fix.

Her grip slipped.

A hair's breadth. Maybe less. But she felt it—the strap shifting, the beam sliding, the walls beginning their slow, inevitable spread.

She tightened her hands. Felt the iron bite into her palms. Felt the blood, hot and slick, running between her fingers.

Hold. Just hold. Someone will come. Someone will fix this. Someone whose hands aren't so tired—

The thought was a surrender. She knew it. But she was so tired. So empty. So sure that there was nothing left inside her but silence and dust.

She held.

The building groaned.

And Petra, alone in the dark, began to break.

19

The building groaned.

Petra held.

Her arms shook. Not trembling—shaking. The kind that meant muscle fibers tearing, tendons stretching past their limits, her body screaming that it could not do this thing any longer.

She held anyway.

The wind howled past the slate tiles. The crossbeam pressed outward, relentless, patient. The iron strap bit into her palms. She couldn't feel the blood she saw slowly dripping down her wrists. The cold was everywhere else. In her fingers. In her bones. In the hollow place behind her sternum where something used to live.

Let go.

The thought was quiet. Reasonable.

Let go. Someone else can fix this. Someone whose

hands aren't so tired. Someone whose song hasn't already—

She squeezed her eyes shut. Forced the thought away.

But it came back. And again. The certainty that she was broken. That she had been broken for months, maybe years, and the valley had finally noticed.

The iron was dead because she was dead.

The Rust was in her too.

~

In the silence between heartbeats, a memory surfaced.

Not summoned. Not chosen. It simply arrived, the way important things do when you stop trying to find them.

Her father's forge. Summer. She was twelve, maybe thirteen, and the heat was unbearable, but she was getting used to it. She was learning to draw out a horseshoe nail. The hammer was too heavy for her wrists. The rhythm was wrong. She kept striking off-center, flattening the iron instead of stretching it.

And she was humming.

She didn't know why. She always hummed when she worked. Some tuneless thing that matched the bellows-breath and the hammer-fall. It helped. She didn't know how, but it helped.

"You're humming again," her father had said.

She'd stopped. Face flushing. "Sorry."

He'd looked at her then—really looked, the way he did when he was about to say something important. His hands were still on the tongs, the iron still glowing between them.

"Don't be sorry," he'd said. "The iron likes it."

She'd laughed. Thought he was teasing. But he hadn't smiled.

"I mean it, Petra. The iron hears something in it. Keep humming."

So she had. For years, she had. Through every nail and horseshoe and gate hinge and cookpot. Through her apprenticeship and her journeying and her return to Wispwater Valley. The humming was part of her rhythm, as natural as breathing.

Until it wasn't.

Until she got tired. Until the last summer, when everything needed to be done right now, and the days stretched too long and the orders piled too high and the work became *work*. Until she started thinking instead of feeling, calculating instead of listening, forcing instead of asking.

She had stopped humming. Sometime in the last year, she had simply stopped.

And the iron had stopped answering.

Emil's music hadn't given her anything. It had only reminded her of what she'd lost. What she'd silenced. What had been there all along, waiting for her to remember.

The iron likes it.

~

Petra opened her eyes.

Her hands were still locked around the strap. The muscles in her arms still shook. The crossbeam was still pressing outward. The Rust was still eating the iron from the inside. Emil was too far away. The wind was too loud. She was alone.

But she wasn't empty.

She had never been empty.

A sound rose in her throat. Not a word. Not a melody. Just a hum. Low and rough and hopelessly off-key.

Strike. Breathe. Strike. Breathe.

The rhythm of the forge. The pulse of the bellows. The heartbeat she'd carried since she was old enough to hold a hammer.

Strike. Breathe. Strike. Breathe.

The iron under her hands shivered.

Not from the wind. Not from the strain. Something else. Something that felt almost like… attention.

She kept humming. The song had no words, but it had weight. It had heat. It had the memory of ten thousand hammer-falls and the smell of coal smoke and the sound of her mother singing

Petra's voice cracked. It didn't matter. The song wasn't in her throat. It was deeper than that. It was in her chest, in her blood, in the calluses on her palms and the ache in her shoulders. It was the song she'd carried her whole life without knowing it had a name.

The Smith's Song.

Not a command. Not a demand. Not forcing the iron to obey.

She was inviting it.

Hold with me.

The words came without thinking. The old tongue. The language her father had muttered over difficult forgings, the one she'd never quite learned but somehow always understood.

Bend with me.

The strap grew warm under her grip. Not hot—warm. The way good iron felt when it was ready to work. When it was willing.

Bind with me.

The warmth spread. Up through the strap. Into the bracket. Across the surface of the iron like sunrise creeping over a valley.

The Rust stopped.

She could feel it—the moment the fear lost its grip. The iron sighed beneath her hands. Not breaking. Not crumbling. Relaxing. Like a muscle finally unclenching after years of strain.

The gray dust shimmered. Stilled. Then, slowly, it sank back into the metal. Drawn down like water into sand, re-absorbed into the iron it had once been. Beneath her palms, the strap grew dense again. Whole. Not new—nothing was ever new—but sound. Solid. Alive.

The strap settled against the beam. The bracket held firm against the stone. The crossbeam stopped pressing outward and simply… rested. The way it was meant to rest. The way it had rested for the past hundred years.

Petra's hands were dull with pain, but she could still feel the iron. The grain of the metal. The memory of the forge fire that had shaped it. The echo of the First Smith's hammer, still ringing in the crystalline structure.

And beneath all of that, a warmth that matched her own.

She jammed Fen's awl into the empty bolt hole. The iron folded around it like clay around a finger, welding itself solid. A new pin. A temporary fix that would hold until she could forge a proper bolt.

If she could forge again.

She could. She would. The song was still there. It had always been there.

She just had to remember to sing.

The wind didn't stop howling. The shutters didn't stop rattling. But the iron didn't move. The strap didn't shift. The bracket didn't slide. The crossbeam didn't press outward.

The building stopped groaning.

Far below, silence. Then a voice—Ferdie, tentative and shaking: "Petra?"

She tried to answer. Nothing came out but a croak.

Her arms dropped. She couldn't have held them up if her life depended on it. The muscles were done.

Completely, utterly done. She slumped against the catwalk, cheek pressed to the cold wood, and shook.

Footsteps on the ladder. Fast. Reckless.

Emil's face appeared at the edge of the catwalk. Pale. Terrified. His lute was gone—abandoned somewhere below. His hands were empty.

He didn't say anything. He just crawled across the plank, ignoring the thirty-foot drop on either side, and knelt beside her.

He touched her ankle, above the boot. He was so warm.

"Petra." His voice broke on her name. "Petra, I couldn't—the music didn't—I thought you were—"

"It worked." Her voice was a rasp. A ruin. But she got the words out. "You reminded me."

"Reminded you of what?"

She almost laughed. It came out as a wheeze.

"That I already knew how to sing."

He stared at her. She could see him trying to understand. Failing. It didn't matter. He would understand later, when she could explain. When she had words.

He reached for her hands. "Let me help you?"

For a moment, she just held onto his hands—both of them, the bandaged fingers and the calloused palms and the warmth that was nothing like iron but somehow just as vital.

She couldn't feel her fingers.

But she could feel his.

20

She woke to the scent of babies. Milk, and wool, and bread-dough skin, and the soft musk of sleep.

Petra blinked at the ceiling. It was too high. Wrong shape. Not her cottage.

The Hall.

She was on the floor in a corner of the Hall, buried in blankets rich with lavender and woodsmoke. Around her, the soft shapes of a half-dozen sleeping infants rose and fell like loaves proving in a warm kitchen. A baby was tucked against her side, its small fist curled around a fold of her sleeve.

She stirred, starting to sit up.

Her body screamed.

The muscles in her arms, her shoulders, her back—every fiber that had held the iron together in the dark—seized in protest. She could feel her pulse in her palms.

Her hands were wrapped in linen bandages, the knuckles hot and swollen beneath.

She settled back down, curling into herself like a child.

The baby made a small sound, protesting the movement. Petra held still until it sighed back into sleep.

The Hall was quiet. Echoey. The chaos of the storm—the crowded bodies, the crying children, the desperate heat of a hundred and a half people pressed together—was gone. Pale winter light slanted through the high windows, catching the dust motes that drifted through the air.

The storm was over. The village was not.

Through the window, she could hear movement outside—dark shapes shoveling, the distant bleating of goats being led to their barn. The animals couldn't wait. Neither could the paths. Life didn't stop for storms.

"You're awake."

Linnea appeared, and then disappeared, and then appeared again.

She lifted the baby at Petra's back and settled them between two others, then knelt down to sit beside Petra. She carried a steaming tumbler that smelled of willow bark and honey.

"Don't try to move," she said. "Your arms need to rest for at least two days, surgeon says. Drink"

"The bracket—"

"Holding. Fen checked at dawn." Linnea slid a hand

behind Petra's head, lifting her enough to sip the tea. "Small sips."

It was warm and bittersweet and exactly what she needed. Petra drank.

"Everyone's out digging," Linnea said. "The pass is buried. Thom's organizing the men to clear the main road. Marda's got the older children hauling firewood."

"I should help—"

"You should lie here and let the little ones keep you warm." Linnea's voice was gentle but firm. The Oracle voice, the one that didn't allow argument. "Your job is done, Petra. Let someone else have a turn."

~

Next time she woke, it was Lenore

The baker carried a basket of rolls, still warm from the oven that Petra had feared would never work again. She set them on the floor beside Petra's blanket nest, then sat down cross-legged, ignoring the sleeping toddler she nearly sat on.

"You roared the roof back on," Lenore said, without preamble. "That's what Marda's calling it. 'The Roar.'"

"I didn't roar."

"You did." Lenore grinned, her sweet face creasing with delight. "Emil said it was the most beautiful sound he'd ever heard. He said you sounded like a forge given a voice."

Petra felt her face heat. "He's exaggerating."

"He's half in love with you." Lenore said it like it was obvious, like everyone knew. "More than half. Here, eat. You need the strength."

Petra's jaw tightened. That wasn't— He was just being kind. They all were. She wasn't going to read anything into it.

She held out a roll. Petra tried to reach for it, but her arms refused to cooperate.

Lenore didn't say anything. She just tore off a piece and held it to Petra's lips.

Petra ate.

It was wonderful. Soft and warm, with a crust that crackled. Lenore fed her the whole thing, piece by piece, then brushed the crumbs from her chin with a matter-of-fact tenderness that made Petra's throat tight.

"Thom's hands are healing too," Lenore said. "Doc thinks he'll be back at the mill in a week."

Petra sighed in relief. "Good."

"He keeps saying he should have done more. That he should have been the one up there." Lenore shook her head. "Men. They always think the answer is more muscle."

Petra almost laughed. It hurt.

"You did good, Petra." Lenore stood, brushed off her apron. "I have to go help Marda with supper. But I'll bring more rolls later. And soup. You need soup."

"You don't have to—"

"I want to." Lenore looked down at her. "Let us, Petra. Just this once. Let us take care of you."

She left before Petra could argue.

A bit later, the baby woke up. The others had all been claimed, only this one remained.

They made a small, questioning sound, then opened their eyes—blue, bright, curious—and stared up at Petra's face.

"Hello," Petra said.

The baby smiled.

Something cracked in Petra's chest. Not breaking. Softening. Like iron heated to just the right temperature, finally ready to bend.

A young mother—one of the dairy farmers, Petra thought—appeared and scooped up the baby with apologetic murmurs. But before she left, she paused.

"Thank you," she whispered. "For what you did."

Then she was gone, and Petra was alone with the blankets and the dust motes and time to count how many muscles ached. Pretty much every one of them.

Toward evening, Emil came.

The Hall had emptied almost completely by then. Most of the families had returned to their homes, their paths cleared, their animals to tend.

Emil stepped over a pile of neatly folded blankets and settled onto the floor beside her.

He didn't speak.

He just reached for her hand—the one that wasn't quite as bandaged—and folded his fingers around hers.

His skin was cold from outside. His hair, damp with

melted snow, was longer than usual. But his grip was warm, and steady, and familiar.

Petra closed her eyes.

She couldn't hear much of the village through the walls. Everyone must be home, an early night after a long day

And she was here. On the floor. Among the blankets.

Held.

She snuggled into his side, squishing the blankets around her. He put his arm around her shoulders, pulling her closer. She breathed in the scent of cold air, pine, and something uniquely Emil.

They sat like that for a long time, not speaking. The fire crackled in the small hearth, the one closest to her, casting dancing shadows on the walls.

"I couldn't hear you," Emil said, finally. His voice was rough. "Up there. The wind was too loud. My lute couldn't—"

"I know."

"I tried, Petra. I played the binding chord, the one that always works, and it just—"

"I know." She squeezed his hand, wincing at the protest in her knuckles. "You were there. That was enough."

He was quiet for a long moment.

"You sounded like my grandmother's stories," he said. "The ones about the First Ones. The ones who sang the mountains into shape."

Petra opened her eyes. He was looking at her—not

with the careful, professional attention of a collaborator, but with something softer. Something that made her chest ache in an entirely different way.

"I was just... remembering," she said. "Something my father taught me. I'd forgotten."

"You remembered when it mattered. Thank you."

She didn't know what to say to that. So she didn't say anything. She just held his hand, listened to his steady heartbeat through three layers of tunic, and let the silence settle around them like a blanket.

Outside, the moon rose. Inside, all was still.

The anchor didn't have to hold tonight.

Tonight, she was held.

21

The morning started with borrowed clothes.

Linnea had brought them the night before —a clean shift, wool trousers, a flannel shirt that with a wide neck and no buttons. "Marda's hand-me-downs," she'd said, folding them at the foot of Petra's pallet, also donated by the innkeeper. "They'll be a bit big, but they're warm."

They were big. The trousers pooled at her ankles, and the shirt sleeves hung past her wrists. But they were clean, and dry, and didn't smell like sweat and smoke and fear.

Petra dressed herself.

It took some time. Her fingers were clumsy, stiff with healing. The trousers were easy enough to pull on, but the shirt was another matter. Just getting her hands down the sleeves was a challenge. But she managed. Shift, trousers, shirt. One piece at a time.

The boots were another matter.

She stared at them for a full minute, sitting on the edge of her pallet in the corner of now-empty Great Hall. Her hands lay in her lap, wrapped in fresh linen. She could wiggle her fingers. She could press them together, feel the heat of her own palms. But grip? Laces? The fine motor control needed to thread leather through metal eyelets?

She slid her feet into them. It would have to do

Soon after, Marda herself arrived, with breakfast.

The innkeeper carried a tray laden with enough food for three people: porridge thick with cream, a pot of honey, sliced apples, a small mountain of bacon. She set it down on the crate that served as Petra's bedside table and stood back, hands on her hips.

"You look like a scarecrow in those clothes," Marda said.

"Your clothes," Petra pointed out.

"My spare clothes. The ones I keep for guests who fall in the river." Marda's eyes crinkled. "Eat. You need meat on those bones."

Petra reached for the spoon.

Her fingers closed around the handle. For a moment, she thought she had it. Then her grip failed, and the spoon clattered back to the tray.

Marda picked up the spoon, loaded it with porridge, and held it to Petra's lips.

Petra ate.

She hated this. Hated being fed like a child. Hated the

way her hands refused to obey, the way her body had betrayed her. She had held an iron strap together with nothing but will and muscle, and now she couldn't hold a spoon.

But the porridge was good. Warm and sweet, with just enough salt. And Marda's face was kind. Practical.

"Fen's coming by later," Marda said, between spoonfuls. "They want to check the bracket. Make sure it's holding."

"It's holding."

"They want to check anyway." Another spoonful. "And Linnea's brewing something for the swelling. Says it'll taste like pond water, but it works."

Petra swallowed. "Everyone's hovering."

"Everyone's grateful." Marda set down the spoon and met her eyes. "You saved the Hall, Petra. You saved all of us. Let us fuss a little."

So she did.

But by mid-morning, Petra was ready to scream.

Fen had come and gone, quiet as always, inspecting her bandages with the same focused attention they gave their pottery. Linnea had arrived with the promised medicine—it did taste like pond water—and had spent twenty minutes adjusting Petra's pillows and blankets until she was "properly aligned with the room's energy flow."

The village children had stopped by in a giggling parade, leaving get-well drawings and small treasures: a smooth stone, a dried flower, a feather from a winter crow.

Everyone was kind. Everyone was helpful. Everyone was so…

Petra wanted to be alone. She wanted to go home, to her own cottage, her own bed, her own silence. She wanted to stop being looked at, worried over, tended to.

She wanted to work.

"You're making that face," Emil said.

He stood in the entryway, stamping snow from his boots. His coat was dusted with white, his cheeks pink from the cold. He looked annoyingly healthy.

"What face?"

"The one that says you're about to bite someone." He crossed the room, sat on the edge of her pallet. "Bad morning?"

"Everyone keeps touching me."

"You nearly died two days ago. People want to make sure you're still here."

"I didn't nearly die."

"You held up a roof with your bare hands during a storm." He tilted his head. "That's at least adjacent to dying."

Petra didn't have a response to that.

Emil looked at her boots, still unlaced at the foot of the bed. Then at her hands. Then back at the boots.

"May I?"

She nodded.

He knelt in front of her. His fingers were quick and

sure as he threaded the laces. Teacher's hands. Used to tying small shoes on squirming children.

Petra watched the top of his head. His hair was too long, curling at the nape of his neck. She wanted to reach out and touch it. But she couldn't reach out and touch anything.

Ugh.

"There." He finished the right boot and sat back on his heels. "Ready?"

"For what?"

"A walk." He stood, offered his arm. "Doctor's orders. Linnea says you need to move, or your muscles will seize."

"Linnea's not a doctor."

"Linnea is terrifying, and I do what she says." He waggled his arm. "Come on. The sun is out. The paths are clear. You've been staring at the same ceiling for too long."

Petra took his arm. It hurt to stand. Every muscle protested, stiff and sore.

It hurt more to stay still.

After Emil had bundled her up in her coat, hat, scarf, and his mittens, they stepped outside.

The cold hit her like a kiss.

Sharp and clean, it flooded her lungs and stung her cheeks. After two days in the stuffy warmth of the hall, the winter air was ambrosia. Petra breathed deep, tasting snow and pine and the faint mineral tang of the half-frozen river.

The village looked like it had been wrapped in white wool and then shaken.

Snow lay in great drifts against the buildings, piled higher than Petra's head in places. The mid-morning sun caught the ice crystals and set them blazing—a thousand tiny fires scattered across rooftops and fence posts and the bare branches of the apple trees. The light was so bright it made her eyes water.

But the main paths were clear. Hard-packed, the work of days of communal shoveling. Emil kept his steps short, not rushing her in the least. Petra's boots crunched on the frozen ground, each step sending a small shock up through her ankles.

The cold seeped through the leather, numbing her toes. She didn't mind. It felt real. Solid. Proof that she was here, and alive, and walking.

Children ran past them, pink-cheeked and laughing, dragging sleds toward the hill behind the schoolhouse. They waved at Emil as they passed. Their voices rang like bells in the crystalline air.

"School's still out," Emil said, waving back. "I told them they could have two more days. The farmers need the help."

"Generous of you."

"I'm a very generous man." He tucked her arm more firmly through his, steadying her over a patch of ice. "Also, I have no lesson plans prepared, and I refuse to improvise in front of twelve-year-olds."

They walked on. The snow squeaked under their

boots, a sound Petra had always loved—the particular music of deep cold. She leaned into Emil's warmth, letting him take some of her weight. His coat smelled of wool and chalkboards and something faintly sweet. Tea, maybe. Or honey.

Strange how natural this felt. How right.

The clip-clop of hooves behind them broke through the quiet.

Ferdie came around the corner, perched on his low, flat delivery cart, reins loose in his gloved hands. His big dappled gelding, Buster, stepped high and proud through the packed snow, breath pluming white in the cold air.

"Smith!" Ferdie called, pulling the cart to a stop beside them. His grin was bright enough to rival the sun on snow. "You're up! You're walking!"

"So everyone keeps telling me."

"Buster loves the new iron!" He patted the gelding's neck. "Haven't had a single slip. Surefooted as a mountain goat."

Petra nodded. She didn't trust her voice.

The horseshoe was holding. No Rust. No brittleness. Just good iron, doing its job.

She filed the observation away. One data point. Too early to celebrate.

But something in her chest loosened, just a little.

Down a ways, Linnea's tea shop and Lenore's bakery, facing each other across the street, were beacons of warmth.

Steam rose from Lenore's chimney in lazy spirals,

catching the sunlight and dissolving into the blue sky. The windows were fogged with heat, but through them Petra could see the glow of the ovens, the movement of bodies, the familiar bustle of bread being made.

The smell hit her before she reached the door.

Yeast and sugar and the deep, caramelized scent of crusts perfectly bronzed. It wrapped around her like a lodestone's pull, impossible to resist. She hadn't realized how hungry she was. How could she possibly be hungry, after Marda's amazing breakfast?

Emil pushed open the door, and warmth flooded over them.

The front room was small but packed. Shelves lined the walls, sagging under the weight of round loaves and braided rolls and something dark and seeded that smelled of caraway. The counter was scarred wood, flour-dusted, with a brass scale and a wooden till that looked older than the building itself.

Through the open doorway to the back, Petra could see the massive brick oven—the beast that had nearly crushed Lenore. Its door was closed tight, sealed by the ugly bent nail Petra had hammered in during the crisis. still holding. Heat shimmered around its edges.

"Petra!" Lenore appeared from the back, flour streaking her cheek, wiping her hands on her striped apron. "You're up! You're walking!" She rushed to the counter, leaning over it toward them. "How are your arms? Does it hurt? Do you want a roll? I have cheese ones—Thom says they're my best yet."

"She wants a cheese roll," Emil said, before Petra could answer.

"I can speak for myself."

"Can you? You were very quiet on the walk over." He grinned. "I thought maybe you'd lost your voice along with your grip."

Lenore was already pressing a roll into Emil's hands across the counter. It was warm, soft, perfectly golden. The cheese had melted into pockets inside the dough, and the top was dusted with herbs Petra couldn't identify.

"For her," Lenore said, "since she can't hold it. Make sure she eats the whole thing. She needs the strength."

Petra opened her mouth to protest—she wasn't a child, she could feed herself, she just needed more time to practice—but Emil was already tearing off a piece and holding it to her lips.

She closed her eyes and ate.

The bread melted on her tongue. Salt and butter and the sharp bite of aged cheese. The herb was rosemary. Rosemary and something else—thyme, maybe, or sage. Each bite was a small revelation, a reminder that the world contained good things, simple pleasures, warmth.

When she opened her eyes, Lenore was watching her with a soft, satisfied smile.

"Oven's working better than before," she said. "I don't know what you did, but the door seals tighter now. Bakes more evenly. The bread rises higher."

Petra swallowed the last bite. "I bent a nail."

"You saved my bakery." Lenore's voice was quiet now, the manic energy fading into something deeper. "You saved Thom." She waved toward the back room, where Thom was nursing a mug of tea.

Through the doorway, Thom raised his mug in silent salute. His hands were wrapped in the same linen as Petra's, but his eyes were clear. Healing.

"You saved all of us," Lenore said.

Petra swallowed. She didn't know what to do with this—gratitude that felt too big for the small front room, for her battered hands, for the ache in her chest that wasn't pain.

"I'll make a proper pin," she managed. "When I can use my hands."

"No rush." Lenore patted her arm across the counter. "It's working. That's what matters."

She pressed a second roll into Emil's pocket—"For later"—and waved them toward the door.

Retracing their steps, they passed the church side gate.

Still broken. One hinge had given way, and the gate hung at an angle, propped open with a rock. Normal wear. Normal rust. The kind that came from age and weather and use, not from whatever darkness had been eating the valley's iron.

Petra made a mental note. Add it to the list.

But the list felt different now. Lighter. This was just normal work. Just repair. Not a losing battle against something she couldn't name.

"You're smiling," Emil said.

"I'm not."

"You are. It's small, but it's there." He bumped her shoulder gently with his own. "What are you thinking?"

"That gate needs fixing."

"That's what makes you smile? Broken things?"

"Regular old broken things." She took a breath of cold air, let it fill her lungs. "Just a gate. Not dissolving. Not dying. Just old."

Emil was quiet for a moment. When he spoke, his voice was soft.

"The Rust is gone. Isn't it."

It wasn't a question.

They walked to the edge of the village, past the inn, before the stables.

The smithy sat at the far end, down where the cobblestones gave way to packed earth. Petra had walked this path a thousand times. She knew every stone, every rut, every frozen puddle.

Today, she stopped.

The smithy door was buried.

Snow piled against it, higher than her waist. The path that led to it—the path that was always clear, always the first one shoveled because Petra needed access to the forge before anyone else needed anything—was untouched. A pristine white blanket, unmarked by boots or shovels.

Petra stared.

"Funny," Emil said, his voice carefully neutral. "They dug out everyone else."

The stables were clear. Both entries to the inn were clear. The schoolhouse, the bakery, the grocer, even the seamstress's shop—all accessible, all shoveled, paths packed down by a dozen boots. But the smithy sat silent and sealed, a white mound against the gray sky.

Petra felt something hot rise in her chest. Frustration first—the familiar, comfortable burn of being kept from her work. Then anger. She needed to get in there. She needed to check the anvil, the forge, the half-finished tools on the cooling rack. She needed—

She stopped.

She looked at her bandaged hands. At the untouched snow. At the village that had, without asking, without telling her, decided to protect her from herself.

"They did this on purpose," she said.

"Probably." Emil didn't move, didn't try to fix it or explain it away. He just stood beside her, solid and warm. "Marda's been organizing the shoveling crews. She has a list."

"And the smithy just happened to be last."

"Seems that way."

Petra wanted to be angry. She tried to summon the fire, the righteous indignation of a craftsman kept from her craft.

But standing there, looking at the buried door, she felt something else instead. Warmth. Love. Belonging.

Not control. Not pity. Just... people who cared enough to make her stop.

"I can't even shovel," she said. Her voice came out smaller than she intended. "My hands—"

"I know."

"I hate this."

"I know."

She leaned against him. He put his arm around her, careful of her shoulders, and they stood there together in the frozen silence. The snow glittered in the afternoon light. The chimney of the smithy rose dark against the white sky, cold and patient.

"It'll keep," he said quietly. "The forge. The iron. It'll all be there when you're ready."

"I don't know how to just... wait."

"You'll figure it out." He turned his head, pressed his lips to her temple—barely a kiss, just warmth, just presence. "You always do."

Her breath caught. She didn't pull away.

The snow squeaked under their boots as they shifted weight. Somewhere in the village, a child laughed. A door opened and closed. Life went on, piece by piece. She didn't have to hold it all together.

Petra, for the first time in months, let herself wait.

22

The smithy came back to life in stages.

First the path. Marda's shoveling crews finally got to it on the third day, four sturdy farmers with wooden blades cutting through the pristine drifts. Petra watched from the inn window, her hands wrapped around a mug of cider, feeling the strange mix of gratitude and frustration that had become her constant companion.

Then the door. Someone—she suspected Emil, though he denied it—had oiled the hinges while the snow still blocked it. When Petra finally pushed it open, the iron moved smooth and silent, gliding like it had been waiting for her.

The forge itself was cold. Dark. The air smelled of ash and metal and—rarest of rare—dust.

Petra stood in the doorway and welcomed it in.

Her hands were better now. Not healed—the skin was

still pink and tight where the forge-song had burned through her, and her grip wasn't what it used to be. But she could hold a hammer. She could work.

The first thing she forged was a hinge.

Not for anyone in particular. Just iron, heated and shaped, the old rhythm coming back to her hands like a half-remembered song. The hammer rang against the anvil—cleaner now, richer, a chord instead of a single note—and Petra let herself sink into the work.

It felt different.

Not wrong. Just… changed. Like a familiar room with the furniture rearranged.

At the end of the first day, she took stock. The anvil, gleaming in the firelight. The tongs, hanging on their hooks. The quench barrel. The coal bin she'd been able to fill by herself that morning. Everything where it had always been.

For once, the odd, empty space by the east wall drew her gaze.

It had always been there. A patch of floor by the wall, cleared of tools and supplies. Sometimes she kept an extra bucket of water there. A few old tools she didn't need. But it had always been empty.

On the second day, the idea came to her.

She was working a set of nails—simple work, repetitive, the kind of thing her hands could do while her mind wandered—when she noticed the silence. Not the absence of sound, but the absence of music.

The forge had always been noisy: hammer-fall, fire-roar, the hiss of hot metal meeting water. But now those sounds felt incomplete. Like a song with the harmony stripped away.

Emil had visited every evening so far. He'd sit on that wobbly tall stool too short for him by the door, lute across his lap, and play while she worked. The Singing Forge, they'd started calling it—though only to each other, only in the quiet moments after the fire died down.

But he always left when she banked the coals. Back to his home across the way from hers. Back to his own space, his own silence.

That stool wasn't enough.

Petra set down her hammer and walked to the east wall. She cleared a patch of floor near the warmth of the forge but out of the path of flying sparks.

Then she started measuring.

It took her three days.

Good wood, seasoned and strong, salvaged from a barn beam that had come down in the storms two winters past. She'd kept it in the lean-to, meaning to use it for tool handles or a new workbench. But this felt right. This was what the wood had been waiting for.

The design was simple. A bench, really—wide enough for a thin man and his lute, deep enough to lean back against the wall. She added a bracket on one side for the instrument, a hook underneath for the case. The legs were sturdy, splayed slightly outward for stability on the uneven floor.

Her hands ached constantly. The burn scars pulled when she gripped the chisel, protested when she sanded the edges smooth. But she didn't stop. Couldn't stop. The work had its own momentum, pulling her forward like the tide.

On the third evening, she oiled the wood with linseed, rubbing it into the grain until the oak glowed warm and amber in the firelight. Then she set the bench in its place by the wall and stepped back.

It looked right. Like it had always been there.

Like it belonged there.

Next morning, a Saturday, Emil arrived early. He carried a basket of rolls from Lenore and a pot of tea from Linnea. He set them on the workbench and turned to say something—

And stopped.

His hand went to his chest. His breath caught—a small, involuntary sound.

Petra watched his face. The surprise. The understanding. The slow dawn of something warm as sunshine spreading across his features.

"You built me a seat?"

"You needed somewhere to put your lute."

"I have the stool."

"The stool's uncomfortable." She crossed her arms, suddenly unsure. "This is better. If you want it."

Emil walked to the bench. Ran his fingers along the oiled wood, the sturdy bracket, the hook where his case would hang. He sat down slowly, testing the height, the angle, the way his back rested against the wall.

Then he pulled out his lute and played.

The first note rang through the smithy, clear and warm.

Perfect

Petra watched him play, her hands aching, her heart light. She turned to the forge and began building the fire.

They worked in a wordless duet.

Not lonely silence—this was the opposite of that. This was two people occupying the same space without needing to fill it with words. The crackle of flames. The soft strum of strings. The occasional patter of hammer on iron, answered by a chord that made the metal sing.

Petra forged a door latch. A set of hooks. A simple knife for one of the farm wives. Nothing complicated. Nothing urgent. Just the steady rhythm of work, with Emil's music weaving through it like thread through cloth.

He played old songs and new ones. He played the jig from that night, fast and bright, and she felt her hammer match the rhythm without thinking. He played something slow and low, and the fire seemed to settle in response, the flames dancing gently instead of snapping.

She didn't ask him to stop.

She didn't want him to.

The day's light was fading when she banked the fire. The coals glowed red through the grate, pulsing like a heartbeat.

Petra hung up her apron, wiped her hands on a rag, rolled her shoulders to ease the ache. Across the room, Emil was packing his lute into its case, buckles clicking in the quiet.

Usually, this was when he left.

Usually, she let him.

"Emil."

He looked up.

Petra didn't know what she wanted to say. She'd never been good with words—that was his gift, not hers. But she knew what she felt. The warmth in her chest that had nothing to do with the forge. The way his presence had become as essential as the fire, as fundamental as the iron.

She crossed the room.

He stood, case forgotten, watching her approach with an expression she couldn't read.

"Thank you," she said. "For staying."

"I don't want to be anywhere else."

They were close now. Close enough that she could see the firelight reflected in his eyes, the faint stubble on his jaw, the way his breath came slightly faster than usual.

She didn't flinch.

Neither did he.

They met in the middle.

The kiss was gentle. Brief. His lips were warm and dry, tasting faintly of Lenore's tea. His hand came up to cup her jaw, calloused fingertips light against her skin, and Petra leaned into him, letting herself be held.

When they pulled apart, his forehead rested against hers.

"Took you long enough," he murmured.

"I'm a blacksmith. We're slow, but steady."

His laugh was soft, breathless.

The fire crackled behind them. Outside, the winter dark pressed against the windows, but in here, the forge was warm. The seat was waiting. The iron was patient.

And Petra, for the first time in longer than she could remember, felt like she had everything she needed.

The forge was hers.

The seat was his.

The song was theirs.

23

Spring

The Wispwater was running high.

Petra heard it before she saw it—that bright, rushing sound threading through the morning air like a welcome-home song. The snow had retreated to the highest peaks, leaving the meadows soft and yellow-green, dotted with the first wildflowers. Crocuses. Snowdrops. The tiny blue stars whose name she could never remember.

She stood in the doorway of the forge and breathed it in.

Behind her, the forge crackled softly. Emil was there, settled into his seat, tuning his lute. The fire was low, just enough to keep the chill off. She wasn't working today. Today was for other things.

"Ferdie's coming," Emil said, not looking up from the strings.

Petra squinted down the path. Sure enough, Buster was clip-clopping toward them, Ferdie perched on his delivery cart with the reins loose in his hands. The little old man was grinning, which usually meant gossip or packages or both.

"Smith!" Ferdie called, pulling up beside the forge. "Beautiful day, isn't it? Makes you feel young again."

"Gorgeous."

He reached into the cart and pulled out a bundle wrapped in butcher's paper. "This came for you. From the capital. Fancy seal on the paper."

Petra took the bundle, weighing it in her hands. Heavy. Dense. Metal, definitely.

She unwrapped it carefully.

Inside, nestled in straw, lay a bar of copper. Not the dull, greenish stuff the valley usually traded for, but something brighter. Purer. It gleamed in the morning light like captured sunrise.

"Test batch," she told Ferdie. "Guild wants to know what I think of it."

Petra turned the copper in her hands. She didn't need to test it—not really. She could feel the quality in the weight, the smoothness, the way the metal seemed to hum faintly against her palms. Clean. Resonant. Whole.

"What do you think?" Ferdie asked.

"It's good," she said. She grinned up at him. "Too good for the likes of us."

Ferdie nodded, satisfied, and clucked Buster forward. "I'll pass it on. Oh—and Lenore says to stop by the bakery later. Something about needing a new piece of furniture. Something small. For someone small." He winked.

"She's…" What was the polite way to say it? "She's, ah, in an interesting way?"

"Very interesting," he said. "Thom's been hovering more than usual."

Ferdie clucked Buster forward. The cart rattled away down the path, leaving Petra standing in the spring sunshine with copper in her hands and a smile lingering on her lips.

She stepped inside the smithy and set the copper on the workbench.

Emil had stopped tuning. He was watching her, lute resting against his knee, that soft half-smile on his face that she had come to know as well as her own reflection.

"Good copper?" he asked.

"Good copper."

"Good morning?"

She crossed to him, leaning against the edge of the forge. The sun had warmed her shoulders. Somewhere in the distance, cowbells rang. The herds were moving up to the high pastures now that the snow had cleared.

"Good morning," she agreed.

He set the lute aside and stood, closing the distance between them. His hand found hers, fingers threading together with the easy familiarity of months of practice.

Months of shared silences and duet songs and a hundred small moments that had built into this.

"Fen's new kiln is finished," he said. "Linnea told me. They fired their first batch yesterday. She was there for the whole thing—wouldn't leave until every piece came out whole."

Petra smiled. "Those two."

"Mm. Linnea's been talking about a joint project. Tea blends with Fen's custom pots. Marda's grandson has already offered to help with the carpentry for a display shelf." He paused. "The whole village is building things."

"Spring does that."

"You do that." His fingers tightened around hers. "You showed them how."

They turned back toward the doorway. Stood together in the sun. Heard the rush of the river, the low of the cows. Inhaled the spring soil and distant hay.

Life going on. Piece by piece. Note by note.

"Petra."

She looked up at him.

His expression was soft. Open. A little nervous.

"If I asked," he said quietly, "what would you say?"

She knew what he meant. The question underneath the question. The future folded into four small words.

"If you asked," she said, "I would say yes."

His breath caught. Then he kissed her—properly this time, not the gentle brush of months ago but something deeper, something that promised and asked and answered all at once.

When they pulled apart, the sun was higher and the forge was warm and the valley hummed with the sounds of spring.

"The valley's in tune," Emil murmured against her hair.

Petra leaned into him, solid and grounded, an anchor and a melody woven together.

"So am I."

ALSO BY ANNIKA STONE

Cozy Fantasy Stories

Tea & Second Chances

Sourdough & Starlight

Green Arbor Touch of Magic Stories

Room for Magic

Room for Light

Room for Dreams

The Room for Magic Trilogy - the 3 books in paperback

Sweet Romance

The Author Next Door

A Taste of Tradition

Lilac Hearts

A Melody for Sunshine

Level Up to Love

Cosmic Hearts

Wild Hearts of Yellowstone

The Christmas Cookie Trap

Winter's Gift

The Valentine's Ruse

ABOUT THE AUTHOR

Annika Stone is the author of over a dozen novels about magic, memory, and the places where our hearts live. Whether she's exploring the complex alt-contemporary emotional landscapes of Green Arbor, brewing up comforting spells in Wispwater Valley, or writing stories of modern love, her work is always rooted in deep feeling and the search for connection.

www.ingramcontent.com/pod-product-compliance
Lightning Source LLC
LaVergne TN
LVHW090937080826
845145LV00003B/784

* 9 7 8 1 9 4 3 1 9 2 9 8 4 *